Charming Blend

A Paramour Bay Mystery
Book Five

KENNEDY LAYNE

CHARMING BLEND

Print Edition

eBook ISBN: 978-1-943420-71-1
Print ISBN: 978-1-943420-72-8

Cover Designer: Sweet 'N Spicy Designs

Dedication

Jeffrey—You charmed me from that very first email!

Cole—Never lose that charming smile, boyo!

Compelling love spells are used to brew up one charmingly delightful whodunit as USA Today Bestselling Author Kennedy Layne continues her cozy paranormal mystery series…

Boxes of delicious chocolates and roses by the dozen are aplenty in the small town of Paramour Bay as Valentine's Day approaches, but all is not so rosy in Raven Marigold's life when a simple love enchantment goes horribly awry. You see, the affection spell is only meant to affect one recipient…not the entire town!

Things for Raven go from bad to worse when small fires begin to break out all around town, causing damages to the local shops and homes alike. What's a witch to do when she believes her attempt at evocation magic might be responsible for sparking these crimes? Why, she must grab her trusty familiar and investigate, of course!

Open your hearts to this spellbinding Valentine's Day tale by falling in love with this charming adventure of mischief, tea, and magic!

Chapter One

"I'VE GOT THIS, my dear Raven. I've got this."

I wasn't so sure that my new part-time helper was telling me the truth. It was the third time this morning that Beetle had reassured me of his competence as a salesman, but the customer in front of us might literally be the third one I lost to the lure of convenient online shopping.

Elsie doesn't even know how to use her cell phone. You're worried about nothing.

My familiar wasn't concerned about anything this morning, with good reason. You see, Leo had been given a hefty dose of catnip by my new and only employee. Don't worry, I had a call into Dr. Jameson to make sure a feline couldn't actually overdose on the intoxicating plant.

Overdose? Nonsense. Where do you come up with this stuff, Raven? Smoking catnip in my pipe is much more relaxing, but I could learn to go down the edible route given time and effort.

If you're wondering how I could hear Leo's thoughts, he and I were linked due to a special kind of magic. I'll have to dive into the details about that after finishing this sale, though. Business at my tea shop had finally been picking up after January's seasonal slowdown, and the incoming cash flow was quite needed and enjoyed.

I'm pretty sure I set a record amount of sales within the first two hours that I'd flipped the open sign over this morning.

It's a pretty sign, too. Don't you think?

"I scan the barcode like so," Beetle murmured in concentration, completely unaware that Leo was utterly enamored by the most mundane things at the moment. Beetle carefully aimed the device with the red laser beams shining forth from the glass cover, biting his tongue as he fastidiously scanned the black lines. His blue eyes brightened with excitement behind his round spectacles when the cash register beeped its recognition. I sighed with relief now that step one had been a success. "Ta-da!"

Look at all the different colors flying by the window outside. Aren't they pretty, Raven?

I closed my eyes and counted to ten, my wish for a quick training session turning into complete fantasy—much like Leo's current view of the cars slowly driving down River Bay.

Not all was lost, though. I might as well take advantage of these ten seconds to catch you up with my life.

Ready?

I'm a witch.

Not a very good one quite yet, but I'm working on it.

Yes, you read that right. You can't tell anyone, though. The residents of Paramour Bay have no idea that the supernatural exists, and it's best we keep it like that.

Anyway, I'd mentioned a bit ago that Leo and I have a special link. He's my familiar. That's not technically true, to be completely honest.

You see, Leo used to belong to my grandmother before she'd dropped dead of a heart attack last October. This tea shop was also hers, along with the cottage she'd left me on the edge of town. I'd inherited both, along with a wax golem by the name of Ted whom Nan thought would be a good idea to bring to life.

Not to nitpick, but it took you seventeen seconds to tell your life story to the reader. I counted on my seventeen claws. Who knew I had so many?

Leo's appearance might be a bit rough, but he does *not* have seventeen claws.

The truth of the matter was that Nan had to resort to black magic to keep Leo from departing this world along with her. Normally, her familiar would have followed her in death. She and Leo had agreed to make the sacrifice so that I could have someone to mentor me. My mother sure as jellybeans wasn't going to do it. She'd done her best to raise me outside of the world of witchcraft.

Nevertheless, the necromancy spell Nan had used had left Leo's orange and black fur with a dreadlock kind of vibe, crooked whiskers, a tail bent like a coat hanger, and a left eye that bulged out just a bit...but rest assured, he did *not* have seventeen claws.

Are you sure? One, two, three...

I sure hoped that Dr. Jameson returned my phone call soon.

"Something went wrong," Beetle exclaimed in frustration, pulling my attention back around to where it should be. He lifted those round spectacles off his nose to glare at the cash register. I peered over his shoulder to see what problem could have occurred, but I hadn't seen what button he'd hit to erase the discounted price. "Something went wrong, my dear Raven."

Raven, help the poor man. I love him, you know. He's my new best friend in the whole wide world.

You should know that Leo didn't actually love Beetle at all. His viewpoint was rather skewed at the moment, causing me to wonder just what kind of catnip Beetle had given my familiar. I hope it hadn't been laced with something that could be fatal.

Whoa, Nelly! Back up the horse cart there. Fatal?

"I'm thinking a new cash register is in order," Beetle suggested seriously before leaning over the counter as if he were conspiring against the universe. Elsie catered to the man's flair for the theatrics by nodding her understanding. "The drawer gets stuck every now and then."

What do you mean...fatal?

I realized that it wasn't easy to ring up the Valentine's Day discount that I'd put on the various tea blends that were available to buy in the shop, but there was absolutely no reason to waste money on a new cash register. Numerous keys had to be pressed in just the right order for the sale to go through correctly. Beetle's blaming the device and his propensity to repeat himself wasn't helping either one of us.

As for Leo, his random annoying comments weren't easing my bad mood in the least. Leo's commentary had only gotten worse since Beetle had been sneaking him a pile of catnip every morning. On the bright side, it had gotten Leo's mind off the glittery kiss mark that a fairy familiar had left behind during one of the previous mysteries we'd solved. For some reason, the glitter on his paw wouldn't come off.

Catnip isn't fatal. I read that somewhere. Are you trying to play a trick on me? I don't think that's funny at all.

"Why don't I ring up Elsie's tea while you go unpack the boxes I brought in this morning?" I offered Beetle a forced smile, hoping my frustration didn't shine through like a beacon. What had I been thinking in hiring a soon-to-be retired tax accountant as my assistant, anyway? I really needed to take one of those self-help classes that made an individual more assertive in life. "Oh, and the herbal remedy teas can go in the storage room. Dee Fairuzo mentioned she'd be by later this morning for her personalized order. Please don't mix them up."

Beetle's frown at being diverted to another project was evident when his weathered features turned downward and his white bushy eyebrows made a rather large V. It was a long story, but he kinda sorta hired himself after spotting the sign I'd taped to the glass door seeking part-time help. He'd been so excited in finding something to do to keep him busy after retirement that I hadn't been able to say no to his rather forceful proposition.

I don't know why. You say no to me all the time.

As it stood, Beetle came into the tea shop for around two hours every morning before walking the two blocks to his own office—where he was in the process of closing his financial advisor and tax services firm.

Trust me, his time with me was a very long, long two hours.

Doesn't Beetle have the best hair? It's like a big, white fluffy cotton ball. I wonder what it feels like.

I guess now would be a good time to tell you that Beetle resembled the mad scientist from *Back to the Future.* You know, after the lightning struck the clock tower. All that was needed to complete the ensemble was a lab coat instead of the grey cardigan sweaters and colorful ties he seemed to favor.

I wasn't that desperate for sales…yet.

"Elsie, thank you for being so patient," I greeted as I took Beetle's place behind the cash register. It felt great to be in my regular spot when dealing with a customer. I took her items and quickly completed her sale. She always paid in cash, so the transaction was relatively simple after calculating the discount. My stress began to fade as I got back into my regular routine. "How was your hair appointment this morning? Did Wilma do something different this time? I swear it makes her look five years younger."

"Oh, she'll be so pleased that you noticed," Elsie gushed, ever so slowly slipping the change into her wallet. Having seen her knobby knuckles, I was always patient when waiting for her to gather her things. It was one of the reasons I initiated small talk. "I've been telling Wilma to go a shade lighter for a year. We watch television, you know. Grey is back for women our age. We've become distinguished just like the older gentlemen have always been."

Elsie and Wilma were known as the dynamic duo of Paramour Bay. The small coastal town in Connecticut was home to three hundred and thirty-five residents, but none came close in personality to these two old hens. And I mean that with total sincerity. They were also my main source of gossip and such, keeping me in the loop on what I should or shouldn't know about certain potential customers.

"I'll be sure to tell Wilma how good she looks before the two of you leave." I packed up the two bags of basic green tea leaves, making sure I didn't forget the chocolate heart I'd been including with each purchase. Personalized touches went far in small towns like these. "What's the chinwag today? I heard that Otis was going to surprise his wife with dinner in the city on Thursday."

"It's one of those fancy restaurants that give you sherbet in between courses," Elsie shared with a nod of approval. "It will make up for him buying his own gift at Christmas. Like that man needed another fishing pole."

"I'd heard that Otis snuck a fishing pole underneath the tree with a tag that read it was from Santa." My laughter bubbled over at the former sheriff's creativeness. "You have to admit, Elsie, that was pretty ingenious. What about you? Are you and Wilma going to hit the town?"

"We're eating at the diner, of course." Elsie finished zipping her purse closed and leaned over as if she were sharing classified information. "Trixie is having the chef serve his special country fried steak, mashed potatoes with gravy, and green beans mixed with pieces of bacon for Valentine's Day. You know that's my favorite meal!"

Hey, Raven. Do I get more catnip for Valentine's Day in the shape of a heart? I'd really like that, I think. Better yet, do you think they have catnip vaporizers yet?

That answer was unequivocally no, but I *had* thought ahead and ordered Leo a very special treat. He would need consoling after he found out that I was cooking a special Valentine's Day dinner for Sheriff Liam Drake. We'd been dating since New Year's Eve, and I'd never been so happy with the current status of my love life.

I winced at the fact that I'd just tempted fate, waiting for the anticipated boom of whatever jinx I'd just placed on Thursday's dinner.

If you had a hit of this catnip, you wouldn't worry about fate.

Thankfully, nothing happened. And fate's ignorance at my provocation had nothing to do with catnip.

Are you sure about that?

"Is Liam taking you out to one of those fancy restaurants?" Elsie asked in her not-so-nonchalant way. I had no doubt that my reply would be around town one second after she and Wilma entered the diner for lunch today. "Or are the two of you staying in for a quiet evening at home? After all, Valentine's Day falls on a weekday. You have to get up early the next morning and be at work."

I take back my previous gift idea. The best Valentine's Day present you could give me is to kick the good ol' sheriff to the curb.

I ignored Leo's dig at my relationship. If you must know, Leo believes that witches and humans shouldn't interact on a personal level.

You're lucky the coven doesn't turn him into a toad. That would fix your wagon.

Trust me, nothing was going to happen given the current state of the coven—which I wasn't even a member of ever since Nan had our family excommunicated for consorting with humans.

"I'm cooking dinner for Liam on Thursday," I replied, turning my attention back to Elsie as I handed her the small shopping bag. Her faraway expression told me that she was either thinking about the country fried steak that was in her near future or the fact that she had some additional gossip to spread around. "And you're right about it being a weekday, so we'll probably call it an early evening."

Did you have to say that? You made the effects of my catnip wear off with that rather carnal vision.

"Raven, dear," Beetle called out from where he was removing items from the box I'd asked him to unpack. He was digging around in the cardboard square with a vengeance. "I don't see anything for Ms. Fairuzo. Did you label her herbal tea order?"

Wilma was peering inside the box as Beetle continued to drag out the packaged items I'd so painstakingly taken the time to add magical elements to last night. If Leo were in his right mind, he'd most likely be explaining that my technique left a lot to be desired.

I wouldn't know where to start. You're a lost cause.

I disagreed, fully believing I was getting better with each enchantment.

Raven, no amount of catnip could make me forget that I still tingle in places I shouldn't.

You see, Nan had a little side business that was extremely profitable. She'd been known around town for dabbling in holistic medicine, and she'd made quite the name for herself. It wasn't just herbal tea for ailments that she'd mixed together, though. What had made her blends so effective had everything to do with the magical enchantments she'd used on them, thereby enabling her success rate to skyrocket.

Oh, I do miss the good ol' days.

I'd carried on the family trade after her death, although my transition had caused a bump or two along the way. However, not this time. Dee had been claiming lately that her husband had lost all romantic tendencies. Another resident by the name of Pearl had gone on and on about the herbal tea Nan had made her to get Henry to fall in love with her, when it was really a charm spell. The two ended up talking about the holistic aid, and I ended up with a new customer for my special concoctions.

Speaking of Pearl, she's back in town with Harold. They just walked into the diner. You know, I'm kinda hungry. Is it too early for lunch? I'm thinking fish, hold the tartar sauce.

Long story short, Nan had passed the herbal tea blend off as an aphrodisiac. Dee had ordered some from me last week to use on her husband, just in time for Valentine's Day. Even Leo couldn't fault my ability to create such a spell. I was rather pleased with the outcome, and now I was eager to see if Dee's husband responded to the charm enchantment.

The diner should start a delivery service. They do that in New York City, don't they? Bring the fish right to your door.

"The package for Dee is inside the heart shaped glass container," I called out to Beetle, walking around the counter so that I could escort Elsie and Wilma to the door. "Elsie, are you heading over to the diner for lunch? I think I'll have Beetle escort you two ladies across the street. That way, he can take Trixie's order of Earl Grey tea over there so that I don't have to make the delivery myself later today."

Do you think Beetle will take me, too? I bet the diner has some fresh cod on the menu.

I was rather pleased that I'd come up with such an idea, because that would have Beetle leaving a bit earlier than planned. There had to be some magical spell I was missing to help Beetle with the learning curve of retail. After all, it wasn't so much different than working with taxes and money all day, was it?

"Had I known you were looking for part-time help, Wilma and I could have pitched in," Elsie whispered, sending my heart racing at the thought of having the two elderly women on my staff. I'd already admitted to my mother that I'd made a huge mistake in hiring Beetle, but I couldn't bring myself to fire him. These two ladies would have sent me to an early grave. "Beetle likes coffee, you know. He doesn't know one wit about tea."

His knowledge for premium organic catnip is all that matters.

My stress that had previously evaporated suddenly returned with a vengeance.

Full disclosure—Beetle wasn't the only one who drank coffee instead of tea.

I lived for the rich delicious beverage, and feigned my love for tea...which technically wasn't good for business. These two kindhearted old ladies wouldn't understand my need for secrecy, so it was best to keep my betrayal under wraps. Soon, I hoped to include gourmet blends of coffee beans and the implements to prepare heaven's perfect beverage among the shop's offerings. Until that time, my preference for coffee was my little secret.

"Beetle certainly makes things interesting around here," I

said with a forced laugh, not knowing how else to sum up my new part-time employee. He was currently holding up the heart shaped glass container with the herbal tea I'd made for Dee, staring at it like he'd never seen anything so beautiful. He really was a sweet man. Guilt flooded my system for thinking it would be best to fire him. I just needed to strive for more patience. "Elsie, what is Wilma doing?"

Why are her cheeks that color? I don't think that shade of red is healthy.

"I'm not quite sure what Wilma's doing." Elsie studied her best friend in confusion. "Is she…blushing?"

The lighthearted flirtatious laugh that escaped Wilma's thin lips was something I'd never heard from her before, but it was the way she'd laid her hand on Beetle's wool sleeve that had me and Elsie gasping in surprise.

Oh, this wasn't good.

I don't ever want to hear that sound again! Raven, these people are ruining what's left of my morning. This falls entirely on your shoulders. Look at what you've gone and done!

"Oh, my," Elsie exclaimed in disbelief, clutching her purse and the bag of teas to her chest as if she'd just witnessed a scene out of an R-rated movie. I was still attempting to rationalize what was taking place in front of us, but I was definitely in a losing battle. "Wilma!"

The thing was, Wilma wasn't paying *any* attention to Elsie.

It was clear the other woman only had eyes for Beetle.

Had this been a normal occurrence, no one would have been shocked to the point of silence. As it stood, there could only be one reason why Wilma was acting in such an amorous way.

It could only be one thing.

Are you proud of yourself now?

Leo was right. This implausible situation was completely my fault, and I had no idea on how to fix it. It was obvious that the love spell I'd cast for Dee had spilled over onto the heart shaped container instead of being imbued into the tea leaves.

I tried to quell my panic.

Good luck with that. Look at those two lovebirds! Beetle just offered to take Wilma for a ride, and I'm not so sure he was talking entirely about using his red VW.

I needed to take that heart shaped container out of their hands before things went from bad to worse. Once it was put into a safe place, I'd have time to go over my options.

I'm not sure how you think things could get worse. This is a low point, even for you.

Leo should have known by now that tempting fate was the worst thing we could do in situations like these. Hadn't we just discussed this? I didn't even have a chance to take a step forward when the smell of smoke wafted from what could only be the storage room.

Hmphf. I thought my vision was cloudy from all the catnip. I guess it's a little late to point out that there's smoke coming from somewhere back in the storage room, huh?

Chapter Two

"ARE YOU OKAY?" Liam asked in concern, pulling me off to the side when one of the firemen came through the opening I'd created in the ivory-colored fairy beads hanging from the doorframe that separated the main shop from the storage room. I didn't want them damaged any more than they already had been by the smoke, so I'd pulled them to one side and tied them off. "I was over at Newt's garage getting an oil change on the truck when your 911 call came through. Chief Mason said the loss was minimal. Mostly smoke damage and some product contamination."

"Yes, I'm fine," I replied softly, though my response was rather automatic. I'm pretty sure I was still numb over what had taken place these past twenty minutes. "I think. I just can't believe something like this has happened."

"It's a good thing you caught the blaze early." Liam nodded to someone else walking through my shop, leaving the floor in dire need of a cleaning. Between the snow and soot, the trail from the front door to the back room was more than evident. "Who knows how far the fire could have spread with the way these shops are connected one after another?"

I'd thought the same thing when I was dialing 911. All I could envision was the entire line of shops on River Bay going up in flames. Thankfully, Liam's trusty dispatcher had answered the phone right away and sent help almost immediately. Between that and the fire extinguisher, I think Beetle and I managed to keep trouble from spreading.

"Eileen had the volunteer fire department here in under three minutes," I said, very grateful that no one had been hurt. Living in a small town certainly had its benefits. "Liam, I don't know how the fire got started. It's not like I have anything in the back that could have generated a spark or gotten too hot. There were no candles and nothing plugged in back there that shouldn't have been. No one was even in the back room, and that's when Beetle and I noticed that the majority of the smoke was coming from the alley. It's a good thing, too, because his briefcase was back there with some important papers for his clients."

Beetle had done me a huge favor and escorted Elsie and Wilma over to the diner after the excitement had died down, though he hadn't balked much considering he fancied himself in love. I still had that mess to clean up, but I was hoping nothing too bad happened while I was dealing with the fire department and this mess.

Technically, an adoration spell didn't work unless there were already underlying feelings between the two people. One couldn't long for what wasn't there to have. It was hard to believe that Wilma had those kinds of feeling for a man twenty years her junior. Then again, I'd seen bigger age differences while living in New York City.

You're assuming that you got that part of the spell right, which at this point is highly doubtful. You really managed to outdo yourself this time, Schleprock.

Drat.

Leo had returned from wherever he'd gone, hopefully to give

Ted a list of ingredients like I'd requested. I was going to need to dispel the magic of my own love spell I'd somehow put on the heart shaped dish instead of the tea leaves. In effect, I had inadvertently created a magical item…a Valentine heart of love.

About that…

"Chief Mason did mention that the fire didn't actually start in your storage room," Liam shared, rubbing his hands up and down my arms. "I had a chance to speak with him after he finished his investigation."

His comforting touch was most welcome. I currently had on a deep burgundy turtleneck that went beautifully with my black skirt and matching knee-high boots, but the ribbed material prevented me from feeling the heat of his hands. He had given me a sense of relief to know that I wasn't responsible for the fire.

Like you're not responsible for the fact that Beetle and Wilma might have run off and gotten married? Who knows what they'll do in that VW if Beetle has a chance to take her for a ride. She's got to be at least twenty years older than that man. She may not survive. Not that there's anything wrong with Wilma robbing the cradle, but she doesn't strike me as the cougar type, if you know what I mean. Listen, getting back to Ted…

"Apparently, the fire started out back of the shop," Liam continued, not knowing he was talking over Leo. I snuck a glance over at Leo's pillow, wondering what he'd been trying to convey about Ted. I really couldn't take any more bad news today. "A lot of smoke leaked through the doorframe and made its way into your shop. Chief is leaning toward someone smoking out back, given that the cold temperatures wouldn't have had anything to do with the fire. It's possible that someone dropped a cigarette in a garbage can and it didn't become engulfed in flames until minutes after the individual had taken his or her leave."

My tea shop was next to the malt shop, but I was relatively sure that Cora and Desmond Barnes didn't smoke. The married couple were the owners and hardly ever onsite, so that left one of their employees. I'd never seen or caught anyone smoking in the alleyway out back, but the only time I ever used that door was to throw trash into the dumpster. Otherwise, that exit was normally locked up.

Could we get back to Ted?

Yes, I really wanted to know what Leo had to say about Ted. Our conversation would have to wait just a moment longer, at least until I got through convincing Liam that I was emotionally okay and that I could manage this small emergency.

"I'll have a look at the back door to assess the damage myself, but you might get away with just a scrub brush to take the soot off the surface. You might want to go through the open products you have back there, too. Smoke has a way of leaving its smell on everything." Liam released his hold on me, much to my disappointment, and took a step back to speak with one of the firemen. "Can Ms. Marigold reopen her shop?"

There was something quite attractive about a man who took charge, and Liam always stepped up to the plate. While the two men continued to talk, I couldn't help but notice one of the other firemen staring at me who been standing next to the cash register. I glanced away, but not before I saw the reason for his interest.

Please tell me that you dealt with the heart-shaped glass container. You know, the root of all of our problems?

I wish I could tell Leo that I'd been smart enough to stash the enchanted glass underneath the counter, but I'd been a little bit busy dialing 911 to make sure my tea shop didn't burn to the ground.

It was becoming essential that Leo get a message to Ted that I was in dire need of those ingredients to dispel the spell. Only witches could hear familiars, so Leo was going to have to get creative in passing along the intended information. If he could manage to figure out how to order organic catnip online, he could certainly get Ted to understand what I needed.

I would if I could, but Ted is currently too busy hugging the mannequin in Mindy's store to pay a lick of attention to my screeching meows. He has an odd problem with her, you know.

A distant memory of Ted carrying the box into the store first thing this morning floated through my mind, but the glass container had been inside the box. He hadn't touched it, so maybe Ted was just paying his daily visit to Mindy's boutique.

Oh, yeah. It's coming back to me. Ted opened the box to check that nothing had been broken on the ride over. You were hanging up your winter dress coat in the back, so...yeah.

The first thing Ted must have set eyes on was the mannequin he fancied through the boutique's window, but golems were usually extremely resistant to magic spells. Remember, he was made of wax. He shouldn't have been affected. He was also six feet, six inches tall, had chipped teeth, whitish blond hair, and resembled Lurch from *The Addams Family*.

Seriously.

Before Ted was Ted, he'd been a wax figure of Lurch.

I know, I know.

My life is rather hard to comprehend.

As for Leo forgetting to tell me that itsy bitsy fact, that had to do with his short-term memory loss.

I thought we established that the necromancy spell your grandmother used on me messed with my memory as a whole. It's not my fault.

Yes. Why yes, we did establish that little detail. And Leo reminding me of that small aspect wasn't helping the situation. I did see the irony here, but I was caught off guard by Liam's defensive reaction.

"Richard, is there a problem?" Liam asked the fireman currently staring at me in a somewhat annoyed tone. He'd noticed the other man's unusual interest in me. I can't say that it wasn't nice to know that Liam had a bit of a jealous streak, but it was definitely wasted on the fireman. His infatuation was nothing short of magic. "Maybe you and I should take a walk outside while Ms. Marigold cleans up so she can reopen her shop."

You've caused an entire town to go insane. I didn't give you enough credit. You are the gift that keeps on giving.

"Raven, I'll be back," Liam murmured, touching my elbow as he passed by. He also whispered something that made me realize I didn't want to spend Valentine's Day with anyone else. "I'll even sneak you a coffee from the diner. Give me fifteen minutes."

The mere mention of hot coffee had lifted my spirits. My smile was genuine as Liam escorted Richard outside, who was currently looking over his shoulder at me as if he wanted to ask for my hand in marriage.

He's in deep, too. Look at that smile.

Oh, boy.

This dire situation needed to be contained fast before someone did something he or she would regret.

And how would you presume to fix something that three random people and a lump of wax have reacted to in the span of three short hours?

"Not everyone has touched the glass container," I whispered

to Leo harshly, not sure if anyone else with the fire department was still in the back room or alleyway. I began to make my way across the shop. "I just need to remove the item from the shop, find a spell in the grimoire to reverse the effects, and then everything goes back to normal."

There might be a slight problem with that plan, and she's entering the store in three, two, one...

"Raven, are you okay?" Candy exclaimed, rushing through the glass door so fast that the bell was still ringing after she'd made her way over to me. I glanced longingly at the heart-shaped glass container. "I heard the fire truck sirens, but I was finishing up an appointment and couldn't leave the salon. What on earth happened? I heard something about a fire."

Go ahead. Tell the Easter egg about your evil design to bring the town to its knees using a love concoction. This should be entertaining to say the very least.

I was beginning to understand Beetle's reasoning on giving Leo catnip every morning.

Hey, don't change the subject. This is all about you and your misguided Cupid's arrow, Miss Dating Game.

Just for the record, Candy Hamilton did not resemble an Easter egg. Her hair was just a reddish orange, with a bit heavy on the orange. Upon second glance, I realized that she'd added a pink stripe to the mix.

Like an Easter egg.

"I'm fine, Candy. Really. Nothing was really damaged, and the fire department got here in time to prevent the fire from spreading to the building. The actual blaze was in the trashcan out back."

Too bad they hadn't been able to put out the flames between Beetle and Wilma.

"Miss Marigold?"

I'd just been about to grab the heart-shaped glass container when Chief Mason came walking through the ivory-colored fairy beads. His yellow hat was a bit askew, but he reminded me of a young Tom Selleck with his thick mustache. All that mattered was that Liam trusted this man's opinion, so I would take him at his word on what he had to say about the fire.

"You can reopen for business, ma'am," Chief Mason said, stepping between me and the cash register. As long as he didn't touch the item that had gotten me into this mess, I stood the chance of limiting its power. "As I told the sheriff, we believe it was simply someone who was careless with their smoking habit."

Some people have no respect for others. At least I keep my special pipe for smoking catnip at the house. I stick with edibles here at the office.

"I appreciate you and your men getting here so fast."

"We're all on a volunteer basis, but we do the best we can." There was a squawk coming from a black radio that was attached to Chief Mason's utility belt. "Excuse me."

I'd spoken with Eileen enough to recognize her voice. I couldn't believe that she was reporting another fire. At least, that's what it sounded like. She and the chief were speaking in code words, but the address given over the little black walkie-talkie was none other than Monty's hardware store.

I hope that Monty remembered the stop, drop, and roll mantra. I tried that during the necromancy spell, you know. It didn't work out for me so well. I'm pretty sure that's how I bent my tail.

Chief Mason didn't even finish our conversation, not that I would have expected him to. He was already jogging through my shop before he ever replied back to Eileen that he and his men were en route.

"I never thought of Chief Mason as being so...charismatic," Candy hummed in an odd manner, tilting her head to the side as she watched the Tom Selleck lookalike through the display window. He'd been in the process of hoisting himself up into the driver's seat when she fanned herself. "Oh, my."

You've broken her poor Easter noggin. As a matter of fact, it's like you gave Cupid a quiver full of little magical arrows and gave him free reign over the town. Good going, Raven. I wonder if we'll make the seven o'clock news.

I didn't have to ask Candy if she'd touched the heart-shaped glass container. The dreamy expression on her face told me everything I needed to know, so Leo's commentary was unnecessary. It was a darn good thing that he'd taught me early on to guard myself against any such spells backfiring. That protection afforded me the liberty to quickly snatch the item in question and store it in a wooden cubicle underneath the cash register where no one could touch it by mistake.

One problem down.

Really? I'm pretty sure that last problem came with numerous steps.

"Candy, why don't we walk over to Mindy's boutique?" I suggested, quickly making my way back around the counter to pat her on the back. "I'm sure she's wondering what happened. This way, I can tell both of you at the same time."

It was my fault that Candy was in this predicament, and I needed to speak with Ted pronto. He was the only one who had the ability to obtain the ingredients I needed to stave off anymore infatuations gone wild. I'd already been closed for the last half hour, so a little longer wouldn't matter in the grand scheme of things.

I've seen that movie where infatuation turns into obsession.

Boiled rabbit? No, thank you!

Leo shuddered in revulsion, sending orange and black hairs flying into the air. I'd hate to see his reaction when he came to the same realization that I had in the last five minutes. You see, coincidence only went so far in situations like these.

Realization? What realization? You can't just walk out of here without explaining yourself, Cupid.

I reached out in front of Candy, pushing open the door for her seeing as she was currently staring after the fire truck as it drove a block down to Monty's hardware store. I breathed a sigh of relief upon not seeing any smoke to indicate the flames had gotten out of control. Hopefully, Chief Mason and his men were able to contain the fire as they had mine.

Did you say coincidence? Raven, don't you dare walk out of here—

I escorted Candy outside, catching my breath when the bitter cold smacked me in the face. Mindy's boutique was only two doors down, but I really should have grabbed my jacket. It was too late now, and I had things to do that couldn't wait a second longer than necessary. I seriously contemplated closing the tea shop for the rest of the day. I'm sure everyone would understand given the circumstances.

That wasn't nice.

Leo had done his vanishing act inside the tea shop and was currently somewhere in my vicinity, not content with the way I'd left things. I was just grateful that he remembered to remain invisible.

Who in the world would be content with the way you left things? You cannot just leave in the middle of a conversation. I would have said your mother raised you better, but we both know that's not the case.

Candy was still enamored with the sight of Chief Mason jumping out of the fire truck and directing one of his men into Monty's hardware store while the other began to unravel the hose. I had a feeling that they wouldn't need something of that strength, and a simple fire extinguisher would probably do.

Why would you think that? What's going on?

"Here we are," I said, thankfully catching Candy's attention. I once again reached out in front of her to open the door to Mindy's boutique. Sure enough, Ted was standing in the corner admiring the mannequin. He was having a conversation with Mindy, but I'd have to cut his talk short. We were wasting time. "Inside you go, Candy."

Thankfully, the hairdresser went inside without any fanfare. I was able to say what was on my mind instead of Leo only getting jumbled thoughts that were more random theories than anything.

You are giving me a headache. Unless it's due to the leftover hangover from all the catnip.

"Leo, I don't think those fires are being set by a person." I swallowed around the lump of panic that had formed in my throat as I continued to watch the scene in front of Monty's hardware store. "I think my spell is sparking flames throughout the town. If we don't hurry in reversing the charm enchantment, I'm afraid that my magic is going to burn Paramour Bay to the ground."

Chapter Three

"ARE YOU IN the hospital or something?"

"No, it's worse," I replied to Heidi's question over the phone. A hand to my forehead didn't help me consider my options any better, but at least I was back in my own shop. Mindy and Candy had bought my reason of cleaning up the floor for dragging Ted out of the boutique. "I think a charm spell I cast—and possibly have messed up—might be responsible for sparking fires all around Paramour Bay."

I'd expected silence, but was rewarded with a laugh. It might have been relief that she didn't have to drive to the hospital. Just so you know, Heidi might have received a call or two when my accident-prone tendencies had gotten the best of me.

If her laugh hadn't been for that specific reason, then we might have a problem. Burning the small town of Paramour Bay to the ground wasn't humorous to me in the least.

"Raven, it can't be all that bad or I would have heard from Jack…who would have received a call from Liam."

She was right. No one had gotten hurt, and the fires had all been minor flare-ups. A little bit of tension released from my shoulders. A best friend had a way of doing that, and I wish I could blink the next two months away.

Me, too.

In case you were wondering who Heidi Connolly was, that's

an easy answer. She was my best friend. Unfortunately, she currently resided in New York City, where she'd been born and raised. She was employed by one of the most prestigious accounting firms, and I was ninety-nine-point-nine percent sure that she was going to take over Beetle's business after the tax season concluded.

Oh, and she totally knew that I was a witch.

It wouldn't have been right to keep her in the dark when she already knew my deepest and darkest secrets.

Going back to your math, adjust that ninety-nine-point-nine percent to one hundred percent. Heidi would never leave me here alone with you. It's a full-time job, and I need breaks. I wonder what all-expense paid resort accepts cats?

In case you hadn't noticed, Leo fancied himself in love with Heidi. She was currently dating a state police detective by the name of Jack Swanson. They hadn't been able to spend time with one another in a week or two due to Heidi's work schedule, but it was nice to finally see her with someone who treated her with the respect she deserved.

Oh, please. He has nothing on me. Once Heidi moves here, she'll see the cat I am through the forest of men. Could we please get back to more important things than Detective Swanson? He's a pretender to the throne. Besides, another fire could wipe out the diner and those cod filets Trixie is serving would be ruined.

I technically shouldn't have called Heidi at the office, but I needed something to take my mind off of the seconds torturously ticking by until Ted was able to gather the various obscure ingredients I needed to reverse the charm spell.

"What did you do?" Heidi asked now that she'd gotten her laughter under control. "And what is a charm spell? Are we talking jewelry or love?"

"Think of Pearl and Henry together," I urged her, unable to stand behind the cash register any longer. I began to pace around the shop, mindful of the high-top tables. The last thing I needed to do was knock the delicate china teapots and teacups to the ground. "Dee was hoping to use the same tea blend I'd created before to reconnect with her husband. I must have accidentally charmed the container I was using to hold the tea leaves rather than the tea leaves themselves. Long story short, Beetle was unpacking the box, he set eyes on Wilma, and it was all over...but the ride in his VW."

Don't forget to mention Ted and his mannequin. That's a mess now, too.

I shot Leo a frustrated glance, wishing he'd go see what was taking Ted so long in finding me those ingredients. We didn't have a lot of time to waste.

While you're at it, you might as well tell her about Candy's crush. I'm not talking about the game, either. You've certainly made a mess of things here.

"Isn't Wilma in her eighties?" Heidi asked in disbelief. "I thought those spells only worked on people who already had feelings for one another. At least, that's what you said before."

"Heidi, you're not helping me." I was beginning to feel like Leo when he became stressed to the point his asthma kicked in. My chest had tightened to the point of pain. "Ted is currently gathering up the components I'm going to need to reverse the spell, but I'm more worried about these spontaneous fires."

"Start from the beginning," Heidi advised, being the true friend she was and taking time out of her busy schedule. "After Beetle and Wilma got all gooey-eyed with one another, what happened?"

"Smoke happened." Was it hot in here or was it just me? Leo

wasn't complaining, so that alone told me the temperature in the shop wasn't the problem. "Apparently, there was some minor fire in the back alley. Smoke seeped into the storage room and then eventually made its way through the fairy beads. I dialed 911 immediately."

"What did the firemen say started the fire?"

"Possibly a cigarette."

"So, the fire may have had nothing to do with your charm spell." Heidi paused, but I didn't bother to fill in the silence. I was too busy keeping an eye on Leo. He'd been awfully quiet over on his heated bed in the display window. "Raven? Am I missing something?"

She looks like an Easter egg with legs, I swear…

I stared out the display window in horror as Candy ran down River Bay chasing after the fire truck. Trying to tell myself that I was still home in bed and this was nothing but a horrible nightmare didn't make anything I was currently witnessing go away.

Look at her run. Who would have thought it was possible?

"Oh, this is bad," I whispered to myself, unable to stop a coat of perspiration from breaking out all over my body. As a matter of fact, I was becoming quite a bit queasy. "Heidi, I need to call you back."

I let the phone slip away from my ear, unable to tear my eyes away from the disaster happening outside on the main thoroughfare. There was no doubt that I needed to put a stop to this disaster real quick.

Hey, there's Richard.

Sure enough, the fireman named Richard who believed he was enamored with me after touching the heart-shaped container was hanging off the back of the firetruck as it drove by the shop.

He was frantically waving at me through the display window with a big smile as if we were more than mere acquaintances.

If I wasn't worried about you being outed as a witch, having the coven descend upon us like a dreaded plague of locusts, and the world basically coming to an end as we know it...I would definitely be enjoying this.

"Go find Ted," I managed to say before my gaze landed on Liam. He was crossing the street holding two to-go cups of coffee. I sure hope he realized that they were both going to be mine. "I'm not going to be able to leave the shop, so Ted's going to have to bring me the grimoire along with the components to reverse the spell."

It's not wise to—

One step was all it took for Leo to vanish into thin air.

I didn't have to be told that taking the grimoire from the protection of the house was a bad idea, but these were extreme circumstances. I couldn't take the chance of anyone else touching the heart-shaped vessel that was currently enchanted with a charm spell. As it stood, I was lucky that Liam hadn't called the crazy wagon for those prominent members acting as if they'd lost their mind.

"What a weird day," Liam muttered, having come through the glass door shaking his head in incredulity. "I'm sorry it took me so long to grab your coffee, Raven. Elsie cornered me in the diner to say that she thought Wilma needed an ambulance for her high blood pressure."

Liam didn't release either coffee to my grabby hands. The black peacock skirt I was wearing had pockets, so I'd already slipped my cell phone inside the right one to allow me the luxury of a two-fisted grip.

My handsome sheriff did one better.

He took the time to come closer and lean down until his warm lips brushed against mine. Time stopped. The intimate moment had me regaining some balance, while somehow causing me to believe that all wasn't lost. My panic slipped away as if by magic.

"I've wanted to do that all morning."

It was well past morning now, but his meaning still warmed me in a way that coffee never could. I inhaled deeply, hoping to keep his intoxicating scent with me to alleviate my anxiety.

"Um, about Wilma." I was afraid to hear Liam's answer for fear that I would be cast as a murderer. It would be my fault if Wilma's heart gave out, and I wasn't one to handle guilt very well. "*Does* she have high blood pressure?"

Liam offered me one of the coffees, not knowing how desperately in need I was for both. I'd have to somehow find a way to convince him to leave the second cup. The rich beverage hitting my tongue was like dipping it into melted chocolate. My insides practically turned to goo.

"Wilma is just fine," Liam reassured me, though he didn't seem totally convinced with his own statement. I understood why when he continued. "Dr. Jameson was having lunch at the counter. It was a bit unorthodox, but he checked Wilma over and decided that she must have had a minor reaction to the new hair dye that Candy had used on her this morning. Wilma even says she feels like a million bucks."

Having a veterinarian check over a human at the local diner was definitely unorthodox. Well, maybe with the exception of Paramour Bay. Worse, poor Candy was being blamed for something that I was solely responsible for.

"It's like something's in the water today," Liam shared with me in bewilderment, shifting so that he could look out the display window. “Chief Mason tried to get out of a conversation with Candy, who’s suddenly taken an immense liking to him.”

“Well, that’s odd,” I said with a nervous laugh. I tried to cover it up with a sip of coffee, but I only ended up sucking the contents down the wrong pipe. Fifteen seconds of coughing and a few pats on the back had me right as rain. “Did Chief Mason happen to say anything else about the fires? I ran into Albert and Eugene, and they said there wasn’t much damage.”

Liam sighed before taking his own drink out of the other cup, erasing any hope I had of siphoning a second serving.

“I’m not happy about it, but I believe we might have a young arsonist with a fresh pack of matches on our hands.” Liam stretched his arm so that the cuff of his jacket wasn’t hindering the face of his watch. “Chief can’t determine how the fires are starting, but Billy Owen was seen running from the alleyway over on Oceanview.”

“Isn’t Billy friends with Sam?” Now that I thought about it, what was Billy doing running around town at this time of the day? “And shouldn’t Billy be in school?”

I’ll explain who Sam and Bill are in a minute.

“Yes—to both of your questions, which is why I’m going to have to cut this short. I called Pete and Sarah, asking them if I could stop by the house.” Liam surprised me by running the back of his fingers down my cheek. His small smile caused my heart to skip a beat, but I was totally okay with that. “I wish I could stay and help you clean up this mess.”

“It’s no problem,” I replied, dropping my gaze to his lips. I wouldn’t mind another kiss. “I’m sure you’ll get things straightened out with Billy’s parents.”

It wasn’t very nice of me to hope that Liam’s investigation turned up that Billy and Sam were responsible for this little arson problem we seemed to be having today. With that said, I had hoped that my wayward craft hadn't taken a nosedive.

"I'll touch base with you before closing time."

One more kiss that was too brief in my opinion, and Liam walked out the shop's door to do his job of keeping Paramour Bay safe. He'd taken the second cup of coffee, but his opinion that Billy might be the cause of the fires had slowed my instant need for caffeine. You see, Billy was best friends with Sam…who worked at the malt shop next door. Could Sam have snuck Billy in the back for a quick smoke? Had it been an accident?

Who am I kidding about my innate need for coffee slowing in light of the circumstances?

I could always use more caffeine.

What did I miss?

Leo suddenly appeared on top of his pillow, looking a little worse for wear. Then again, that was par for the course. I sure was glad to see him, though. His presence meant Ted was on the way to the shop with my ingredients and the Marigold family grimoire.

"You missed a lot." For the first time since this morning's incident, my outlook wasn't so dire. "Leo, I might not be the one causing all the fires around town. Liam mentioned that he thought Billy and Sam might be responsible for the damage. Billy is a year younger and should be in school right now, but someone said he was seen running out of the alleyway behind Monty's hardware store."

Good. Then there's nothing for us to do besides free Beetle, Wilma, Richard, and Candy of this charm spell gone wrong. Easy-peasy. I'll be home smoking my catnip pipe by dinnertime tonight.

"Not so fast," I cautioned him, unable to just ignore what had taken place this morning. "Leo, a lot of us shop owners might have been out of business had those fires not been contained so quickly."

Don't even think about it. I already told you that I have plans, didn't I?

"We've solved murders and even a kidnapping case. Helping Liam with an arson investigation isn't that far out of our wheelhouse. We can even—"

My suggestion of using magic to aid in the arson problem happening in Paramour Bay had been cut off due to the sirens of our one and only fire truck. The large red vehicle drove past the shop quickly with Richard once again smiling and waving from his place on the back bumper.

What was even a worse sight was seeing Beetle and Wilma following close behind in his red VW bug as they chased the fire truck.

Raven, you certainly do have a way of jinxing fate, don't you?

Chapter Four

"THERE WAS NO real damage done to Beetle's house," Liam said over the phone, the wind blowing against the mic making him somewhat hard to understand. I got the gist of what he was trying to relay to me, though. "Listen, I've got to go. I'll call you later tonight."

"Be careful, please."

I'd begun to end each phone conversation I had with Liam with those three words. With him being the sheriff of such a small town where the most serious crime was usually speeding down the main thoroughfare wasn't exactly the most dangerous work, but there was always the chance of more serious offenses that could creep up every now and then. Complacency was the worst enemy of every law enforcement officer anywhere.

Like the rash of recent murders, attempted thefts of items of value…and now arson. No matter what Liam was being paid to keep the citizens of Paramour Bay safe and sound, it certainly wasn't nearly enough to risk his life.

There's not enough high grade premium catnip in the world to get me to even mildly contemplate the idea of that thankless job. On top of all the man's stress, he has to deal with Eileen…and your tomfoolery. But I feel his pain in the latter. I'm sort of a first responder in that regard. No wonder I need my pipe.

"Where has Ted gotten off to?"

You've asked that already. Twenty-three times in the last hour, to be exact.

"You said Ted was on his way here with the grimoire and the material ingredients I'd need to reverse the spell. That was over an hour ago." I slapped my phone against the palm of my left hand, considering my options. There was only one thing I could do. "I'm going to have to go out and look for him."

It was going on two o'clock in the afternoon. Hours had passed since the first incident, which was way too long to allow a misguided charm spell free reign to do its damage amongst the general population.

"I need to be proactive here."

I hate to say this, but I think you need to—

"Not one word about calling my mother," I cautioned with a piercing stare Leo's way. She was always his last resort—his eventual fail-safe answer to all my mishaps. I mean, I was scraping by my lowest of the lows, and I couldn't blame him. "Mom has had to clean up too many of my messes recently. I can't bear the look of disappointment any more. I will reverse this charm spell, as well as figure out who or what has been starting the fires all around town."

You might want to look in the mirror, in that case.

"You're probably right," I conceded slightly, although not completely. Leo did have a legitimate point. "*But,* there could be an actual arsonist out there. Coincidences do happen, you know. It's possible."

I quickly made my way to the back room which still had the string of ivory-colored fairies pulled to the side. My dress coat reeked of the greasy, smoky smell of burnt garbage, but there was nothing I could do about the odor until I got the chance to drop it off at the cleaners. There was certainly no time for that kind of errand now. I grabbed my dress coat from the small hook on the wall before quickly walking back to the cash register.

Are you seriously going to go look for Ted?

"Yes. What else can I do?" There was a small cabinet underneath the cash register where I kept my purse during open hours. It didn't take me long to rummage through my bag and locate my car keys. "What if he fell into a snowbank or something else bad happened?"

Ted liked the walk to and from my cottage to town. Just because he was a wax golem didn't mean something bad couldn't happen to him. In fact, it made it more likely.

Ohhhhh. I get it. Fires. Arson. Ted could be a pool of melted wax somewhere, just chilling.

"Stop that nonsense," I admonished, unable to get such a horrid vision out of my mind. "Nobody has melted Ted, and he's not chilling anywhere. Let's just take a drive and see what's taking him so long to get here."

I should stay behind. You know, in case Ted shows up in a lump.

I wasn't going to lie to you. The length of time that had gone by since Ted had been in contact with either me or Leo was rather disconcerting. Usually, Ted was either in the shed out back of Nan's old place on the edge of town or at Mindy's boutique looking in the window. Leo had already checked both places around fifteen minutes ago.

Ted was nowhere to be found.

"I see that small pile of catnip in the corner of your bed," I pointed out before slinging my purse over my shoulder and heading toward the door. "You can wait to light up until after we come back and clear up our little mishap from this morning. Oh, and Dr. Jameson called—he said that he's never heard of a cat overdosing on catnip. Of course, most cats don't smoke a pipeful of the stuff."

Well, what does he really know? The day is finally looking up! And don't think I missed your "our little mishap" comment. This is all on you, Cupid. All on you.

With the way my luck was going, Leo would end up in some veterinarian medical journal somewhere soon as the first feline to ever go into a catnip-induced catatonic state.

But what a way to go...

"I want to make one quick stop before we get in the car," I said rather vaguely, hoping to get out of the shop before Leo realized my destination. "I'll meet you there."

I was able to make it through the door before Leo grasped my intentions, but he managed to stop me when I was inserting the key into the lock. I'd never reopened for business today, so I hadn't needed to worry about the sign or when I'd be back.

What destination? Where are you going? Why are you being so cagey?

Leo wasn't visible, but that didn't stop him from pummeling me with an endless supply of pointed questions. I couldn't blame him, really. It was his job to help guide me along this witchcraft journey, and I certainly wasn't making it easy on him.

Abbie and Gillian were walking into Mindy's boutique two storefronts down, so I just smiled and pretended not to be able to answer Leo. Sure, he could read my thoughts, but I'd kept my mind as clear as I could so that he wouldn't have a complete meltdown.

Meltdown? Raven, you're raising my anxiety level precipitously.

I'd taken maybe ten steps before opening the front door to the malt shop.

Leo made sure that his wheezing was loud enough for me to

hear him over the fifties music coming from the speakers on the jukebox. I ignored him as I crossed the threshold, allowing the door to close behind me. The warmth inside encased me with open arms.

I'd been inside the malt shop a time or two with Heidi, and the décor instantly took the customer back to a simpler time of the 1950s. The red and white checkered scheme was heavy throughout the shop, even having the red leather stools lining the counter for where patrons could drink their chocolate milkshakes or eat their over-loaded banana splits.

Cora and Desmond certainly went the extra mile on every aspect of their menu of classic malt shop fare. Extra toppings were the standard for every order. The staff even put an official Milk Magic Flavored Straw in every malt and milkshake, which came in four flavors—chocolate, strawberry, vanilla, and cookies & cream.

The large round speakers flanked the stylized base of the jukebox in the back of the shop that was hard to miss considering the pink and blue neon lights. The old forty-five records that were displayed in an arc across the top of the machine were just window dressing. The electronic menu screen held several thousand possible song selections, encompassing the top forty songs of the weekly roundup for the past five decades.

To top it off, the young man behind the counter was wearing one of those soda-jerk paper hats with a matching white cotton apron.

"Good afternoon, Miss Marigold," Sam greeted, a big smile on his young face.

See? Sam looks innocent enough. Let's go.

Leo had decided to join me, after all. I'd become rather efficient at listening to him yammer on and on in my ear while simultaneously having a conversation with someone else.

"Hi, Sam," I replied, readjusting my purse strap as I walked closer to the counter. I hadn't given this enough thought. "Um, could I please have a chocolate malt, with a cookies & cream straw please?"

It's thirty degrees outside. Would you like to change into your swimsuit, too?

The malt shop stayed open year-round, but that was because they didn't only serve malts, milkshakes, and ice cream. The menu also offered bacon cheeseburgers and fries, which in all honesty was better than the ones served at the diner. Besides, little ones didn't care how cold it was when it came to eating ice cream.

What I needed to do now was to keep Sam busy while I nonchalantly asked him questions about Billy.

I hate when you transform into Nancy Drew.

"Yes, ma'am. One chocolate malt coming right up."

Sam didn't waste time. He even twirled the tall metal container in his hand that he would use to mix the ice cream, malt powder, and other ingredients. It was easy to see that he was very proficient at his job as a soda-jerk.

How did we end up with Beetle again?

"Sam, was there any damage to the rear of the malt shop from the fire?" I asked, figuring that was a question that any other shop owner would ask, given the circumstances. "I had some smoke damage, but nothing major. I did lose a little bit of open inventory in the back room, though."

Smooth. I'm impressed. In the meantime, Ted could be freezing into a block of goo as we speak. Could we please go now?

"The trashcan was closer to your side, so we didn't even know there was a problem until we heard the sirens." Sam had already scooped the chocolate ice cream out of its bucket and was in the process of adding in the other ingredients. I was running out of time. "Did you hear about the other fire over at Monty's hardware store?"

Perfect. Sam had given me the textbook opening.

You're manipulating a nineteen-year-old. Way to go, Raven. You're a true inspiration.

"I did hear about Monty's shop." I stepped closer to the counter and raised my voice so that Sam could hear me over the whirl of the blender. "Aren't you friends with Billy?"

"Oh, Billy didn't have anything to do with those fires," Sam said, instantly coming to his friend's defense. He was even shaking his head rather emphatically. "He was just using the shortcut through town to get to his house. Besides, he has a crush on Bonnie. He stops in here whenever he can to see her when she's at work."

Such loyalty. You could take lessons from this kid, Raven. He hasn't got a devious bone in his entire body.

"Billy is supposed to be in school, though, isn't he?" I rummaged through my purse so that I didn't overshow my interest. I eventually pulled out my wallet, only to find Sam eyeing me warily. "Oh, I wasn't trying to suggest that Billy was guilty. I was just thinking that if he was using the shortcut, do you think he could have seen who was responsible for starting the fire?"

Nice recovery.

"Billy is a senior," Sam explained, expertly pouring my chocolate malt into a tall to-go cup. "He only has morning classes and then attends his internship with one of the teachers over at the elementary school. There was a substitute for the teacher's class today, so the school sent him home early."

There you go. Case closed. You're the culprit, Raven. Just plead guilty and throw yourself on the mercy of the court.

When Leo put it like that, I didn't come across as a very good person trying to pin arson on a teenager.

Wow.

Maybe I had sunk to a new low.

The bell above the door chimed behind me. I turned to find one of my not-so-favorite people walking in like she was walking down a runway, modeling an expensive dress coat and hat.

Ohhhh, a feather.

Leave it to Leo to spot a feather in the emerald green hat that was atop Cora Barnes' perfectly styled hairdo. I could only pray that Leo could restrain himself from attacking the accessory perched upon the top of her head.

"Good afternoon, Raven," Cora greeted, the wide arch of her eyebrow exaggerated as she looked me up and down. She motioned for the young girl who'd entered the shop with her to proceed. It was Bonnie, and apparently the one Billy had a crush on. She was one of two shift managers here at the malt shop, and she didn't look all too happy to be dealing with her boss. I couldn't say I blamed her one bit. "What brings you in today? Are you here to talk about the fire? Bonnie came down to the ladies auxiliary meeting to reassure me there was no damage done to our storage area, but I've obviously come to check for myself."

Had the feather in Cora's hat moved just a bit?

Maybe…a little. It might be alive.

Neither Leo or I were too fond of Cora, but that was due to her dislike for my mother. To be honest, Cora had apologized to me over a month ago for her animosity. Of course, that regret didn't encompass my mother. Cora had basically extended an olive branch my way, but it was hard not to crush those suckers and spit out the seeds at her feet.

"I just came by for a chocolate malt." I gave a small shrug, hoping I came across convincing enough. "I'm heading home to grab some supplies that will help take away the smell of smoke in the back of my shop, but I needed a little chocolate fix. As it happens, Sam and I were just talking about the fires happening all over town, though. Billy may have seen someone in the back of the alleyway of Monty's hardware store on his way home."

"Paramour Bay has seen quite a lot of odd things over the past four months," Cora conceded, but she'd purposefully been passive aggressive with the timetable. It so happened that I'd moved to town last October. "I do hope that Liam finally discovers the root of the problem before it's too late."

I wasn't surprised in the least when Cora's hat went sailing off her head.

I blame the bird in her hair.

Cora made a frantic grab for the emerald green fedora and managed to catch it before it landed on the black and white checkered tile. She checked it all over before setting it securely back on her head.

"I was never one to be able to keep a hat on my head, either," I said with a crooked smile, hoping to cover up Leo's spiteful reaction to her choice of accessories.

"We just saw Billy enter the police station with his parents," Bonnie offered up, ringing up my malt as Sam finished spraying whipped cream on top, then carefully placing the round lid overtop the creamy mound and popping a cookies & cream flavored straw through the circular opening. "Mr. and Mrs. Owen didn't look very happy they had to leave work and bring Billy into the station for questioning."

"Billy was inside when the fire out back happened, so I know he wasn't responsible," Sam protested, clearly wanting to defend his friend. "We never left the shop to go out back, Ms. Barnes."

Once again, all roads lead to you, Raven. Poor Ted is probably a frozen crayon sticking out of some snowman's face by now.

"Well, then," Cora declared, as if Sam's claim of innocence was all she'd needed. "I'll take a quick look out back to confirm there's no damage to our side of the building and then be on my way. We're voting on whether or not the ladies auxiliary will be hosting its annual Easter egg hunt in April. It's just a formality. We've hosted it every year for the past decade."

Candy's run down River Bay must have been a reminder.

Bonnie rolled her eyes as she took my ten-dollar bill, quickly making change and handing me back a few ones. Apparently, Cora had raised the prices on her malts. I should have checked the menu out before ordering. With that said, I stuffed a one dollar bill into the tip jar.

Hey, that could have gone to my monthly subscription to Catnip-Times magazine. There is such a thing, you know.

"Thank you, Miss Marigold," Bonnie said, closing the cash register and sliding a napkin across the counter next to my malt that Sam had just set down. She glanced over her shoulder to make sure Cora was out of earshot. "The winter months are always slow. I tried to talk Ms. Barnes into holding the ladies' auxiliary meetings here, but she adamantly refused to subject those proper ladies to a malt shop."

Uh, Raven?

Bonnie was a sweet girl in her early twenties. I didn't know much about her other than she was taking some online college classes and working at the malt shop during the weekdays. I could only imagine how hard it was for Cora to keep an experienced full-time manager on staff.

Roger Aimes was the more senior shift manager, but I'd heard from Elsie and Wilma this morning that he'd gone home early with the flu. It was that time of season.

Paramour Bay was a small town, and most everyone drove into New Haven for decent jobs. It wouldn't be long before Roger and Bonnie left here for greener pastures.

We might have another problem.

"Don't give up the effort," I suggested when what I really wanted to say was that Cora wasn't using her brain when it came to business. It wouldn't have been nice of me to talk bad about another shop owner, especially to one of her employees. Besides, Leo had distracted me with his comment. I really couldn't handle another problem right now. It wasn't like I heard any more sirens. That was a plus, right? "You two have a great day."

Sam and Bonnie both waved, but their gazes weren't on me. They were focused on the door behind me.

It's like directly out of a horror movie. Whatever you do, don't turn around.

It wasn't like I could stand at the ice cream counter for the rest of my life, and there were things that had to be done. Number one on that list was reversing the charm spell so that this town could get back to normal. So, whatever or whoever was behind me would have to be dealt with.

Don't say I didn't warn you.

It was a good thing I hadn't taken a sip of my malt before turning around. I would have choked to death otherwise. My worst nightmare was standing on the sidewalk, all but glaring at me through the glass door—my mother.

And her glare was lethal.

It wasn't me this time. I swear. It was all her.

Chapter Five

"WHAT ARE YOU doing here?"

"The better question to ask is *why* am I here," Regina Lattice Marigold muttered underneath her breath while I unlocked the tea shop so we could both get inside where it was warm. She'd begrudgingly accepted the malt from my hand so I could fish my keys out of my purse. "I was minding my own business this morning when I got an unsettling impression that all was not right in the little town of Paramour Bay. My life has been sailing fairly smoothly lately, despite your best efforts to keep me from enjoying the latter years of my life."

That means you, Raven, in case you didn't know where your mother was going with that little innuendo.

"When you didn't answer your phone, you left me little choice but to drive the two hours it takes to get here."

Tell me you didn't left swipe her, Raven.

I might have swiped a phone call…or two. In my defense, I'd been a little busy this morning. Okay, I swiped four times, but that was only because I was a horrible liar and she would have figured out something was wrong.

It's a good thing your grandmother can't fire me. I'd have been unemployed and left for dead long ago.

"Would either one of you care to tell me what's happening here?"

Both Leo and I remained silent as we all entered the tea shop, but it wasn't like I could prevent my mother from detecting the aftermath. After all, the smell of smoke hung heavy in the air. I snagged my malt from her gloved hand before she could drop it and took a fortifying drink of the thick chocolate substance. It wasn't coffee, but it would do in a pinch.

If you're getting your caffeine, then I'm eating the rest of those edibles Beetle left me this morning. Fair is fair.

"Oh, my word! What on earth happened here?" My mom quickly ascertained that the shop was still standing, but her gaze did land on the ivory-colored fairy strings pulled back on one side of the doorframe. "Did you set fire to the storage room? Please tell me that you weren't casting—"

"I was not casting a spell in the back of the shop, Mom," I defended myself, leaving out that I did have a habit of casting smaller incantations on the tea leaf blends for my holistic customers on occasion. There was no need for my mother to know every little detail about my life. Even young adults deserved their privacy. "There was a small fire in the back alleyway. The garbage can had been left right next to the door and the smoke seeped in. Unfortunately, there is quite a bit of smoke damage. It could have been much worse."

"So, no one went to the hospital?" My mother untied the belt around her waist before unfastening the buttons on her dress coat. It wasn't like I could send her back to New York City after that long drive, but I was tempted to send her over to the cottage. "Raven, if no one was hurt, why did I get the feeling that something was horribly wrong here?"

Don't answer that question. It's a trap. Your mother is so good at interrogating the unwitting.

"Leo, are you suggesting that my daughter shouldn't answer

me?" My mother arched her brow in that holier than thou way she'd perfected. "Why is that?"

I plead the fifth...and any others that might apply here in this instance.

"Fine," I grumbled, knowing this was a losing battle. "I cast a spell that might have gone off the reservation. It's nothing I can't fix with the proper material ingredients."

The thing about staring at my mother was that it was like looking into the future in twenty-three years. We were practically the spitting image of one another, minus a couple of wrinkles and the fact that we had completely different sense of styles. Mom favored the more classic sophisticated look, while I took after Nan with a more whimsical flare of a modern witch.

You know, maybe it's the addition of that whimsical flare that always gets you into trouble.

"Mom, why don't you go on over to the diner?" I suggested, hoping to get her out of the way so that I could finally locate Ted and take care of my minor mishap. "It's in the middle of the afternoon, and I haven't even had lunch. Grab us a table, and I'll be over there shortly."

"What exactly do you mean that a spell went awry?"

The fact that my mother had taken off her dress coat told me that she had no intention of going anywhere anytime soon. She even set her purse down on one of the high-top tables before draping her coat over the seat of one of the matching stools.

"It didn't go as planned, but it'll be an easy fix."

You're getting better at fudging the facts, I'll give you that.

"Leo, you aren't helping my cause," I exclaimed, glaring at him when my mother disappeared into the storage room. "Mom can hear every word you say, so eat your edibles and keep quiet!"

I believe the two are mutually exclusive. If I thought I could have the five minutes it would take to enjoy my snack, I would. Unfortunately, our afternoon is about to go from bad to worse. Wait, that already happened. From worse to…hey, Raven, what's worse than a complete disaster?

Sure enough, Ted came sauntering through the shop's door as if I hadn't been waiting anxiously on him for hours. He wore his usual suit, along with the long black coat I'd purchased for him to ward off the bitter winter winds. The cold temperatures didn't harm him in any real manner. It just slowed him down on the odd occasion. Besides, it would have seemed rather odd for him to go walking around town without something warmer than his suit jacket on while moving at a snail's pace.

What is your mother doing back there? She's taking a rather long time just to survey the damage.

"Ted, where have you been?" I whispered, taking the basket of ingredients I'd asked for so that I could reverse the charm spell. I, for one, was grateful that my mother hadn't returned from her little trip out back just yet. It gave me time to hide the basket. "Leo has been looking everywhere for you. We thought—"

"Mr. Beetle offered me a ride," Ted replied in his typical monotone manner, not bothering to expand what he meant by his answer.

I quickly walked around the cash register so that I could store the basket next to the heart-shaped glass container. Both were now together, and it wouldn't be long before everything returned to normal.

I'm not so sure about that. Who is your mother talking to back there?

"What do you mean, Beetle offered you a ride?" I asked, just now realizing the consequences of Ted's statement. My mother could wait. "We saw Beetle and Wilma following a fire truck to his residence around an hour ago. There had been a small fire at his house, but the fire department was able to get the flames under control."

"You didn't let me finish," Ted explained, stopping when a few choice words came drifting from the alleyway.

"Ted, focus."

I'd share my edibles...if there were any left.

"I told Mr. Beetle that I didn't need a ride," Ted clarified, frowning when it was clear that my mother wasn't the only one offended. "Miss Raven?"

Ted wasn't one to mince words, and I got the gist of his question. He wanted to know what I was going to do with my mother, who apparently had run into Cora Barnes out back. There was only one person in this town that riled my mother to that extent, and that was definitely Cora.

Ted still hadn't explained what had kept him so long, but I couldn't allow a catfight to erupt between my mother and her nemesis while I fiddled with Rome.

You could, but I guess that would invite that karma you want to keep away, wouldn't it? I'm beginning to think you're a little late on that front. Karma, meet Raven. Raven, meet Karma. Two ships that crash in the night.

"You aren't funny, Leo," I muttered, glad I hadn't had time to remove my coat. I made my way through the storage room and out through the open door to the alleyway. Sure enough, my mother was making a ruckus. "Mom, what on earth is going on between the two of you?"

"This...moneygrubber...believes you're the one responsible for the fire," my mother all but bellowed before leveling Cora with a look that might not kill, but would certainly maim. It was a good thing my mother had sworn off witchcraft. I wasn't so sure Cora would come out of this confrontation unscathed, as it were. Then again, my mother's definition of giving up magic had a lot of somewhat sketchy loopholes. "You can take your opinion and—"

"Cora, you know very well that I didn't have anything to do with the fire," I clarified, pretty confident in what Cora had been suggesting with her accusation. My mother just wasn't one to turn the other cheek. Neither was I, but there were times it was better to walk away than draw attention to one's self. "Chief Mason has had to attend two other fires this morning, and he believes it is the work of an arsonist."

"It was your mother who first suggested that one of my employees could have been the culprit," Cora shared, the two women now in a staring contest. "Sam has assured me that he and Billy did not set foot in this alleyway to smoke cigarettes or anything else."

"And I believe Sam, especially since there was another fire at Monty's hardware store shortly thereafter." I slid my hand through my mother's arm to hide the fact that I poked her side. She knew better than to engage with Cora. "I'm sure my mother didn't mean anything by asking her questions."

"Bonnie doesn't smoke, either," Cora tagged on defensively, wanting to ensure that I didn't blame her young manager, either. Cora glanced down the long alleyway, both of us coming to different conclusions. I saw an opportunity for almost anyone to be the guilty party, but Cora had to go and make it personal. "From what I've gathered, Beetle has been acting exceedingly strange this morning. Was he inside with you at the time of the fire?"

I tightened my grip on my mother's arm when she moved to

take an aggressive step forward.

"Beetle was with me, along with Wilma and Elsie. Cora, there are a lot of shops along this alleyway. Had this been one occurrence, I could agree that maybe someone had been smoking and tossed a cigarette butt into the trashcan without thinking about it." The fact that two other fires had taken place within hours of each other told a different story. "I think Chief Mason is right about someone out there purposefully settings these blazes. We're just lucky this one was caught before any real damage was done."

"Mrs. Barnes?" Sam poked his head around the back door to the malt shop. "Your husband has been trying to reach your cell phone. When you didn't answer, he called the shop's phone. He's on hold now."

Cora didn't even bother to say a word as she turned on the high heel of her dress boot and followed Sam inside her place of business, slamming the steel security door and turning the bolt with an audible click. I would have loved to say the tension from such a confrontation eased from my shoulders, but I still had my mother to deal with…and it wasn't like I could send her back to the city without first taking care of the business at hand.

"You'll be pleased to know that I now have the ingredients to reverse the charm spell that didn't go quite as planned," I offered up, instinctively stepping away from her and toward the door. "Like I said earlier, go ahead and grab a table at the diner. I'll take care of this itsy-bitsy snafu so that we can enjoy a nice meal before you return to the city."

"Charm spell?"

Drat.

I'd been so careful to avoid saying what type of enchantment had gone awry.

"It's not that big of a deal, Mom."

I quickly made my way back inside, not bothering to wait for her. She could close the door behind her, but I wanted to reach the front of the shop before she did. That way, I could send Ted on his way before she could trap him and ask more questions. Ted had a way of blurting out the truth without thinking of the consequences.

Sure enough, Ted was still in the shop when I came through the doorframe free of beads. Unfortunately, he and Leo were staring out the display window as if a parade was marching down River Bay.

"Please, please tell me that nothing else has happened," I practically begged, not even taking the time to remove my jacket as the sound of sirens began to get louder with each passing second. I simply ran to where they both stood, joining them in staring out the window at the spectacle in dismay. "This can't be happening."

"Raven Lattice Marigold."

You're in trouble now. Mommy knows what you've been up to.

I cringed when my mother clearly saw the sight before us—a red fire truck with a waving and smiling Richard, Beetle and Wilma following behind in his red VW...and Candy in the backseat.

"What have you gone and done?" my mother whispered in horror, placing her hands on either side of her face in disbelief.

Regina, have a seat. This explanation might take a while.

Chapter Six

"THE REPORTS OF another fire were a false alarm," I exclaimed with relief, tucking my cell phone into the pocket of my skirt. Liam had not only made my day bearable with caffeine, but he'd also made the next few moments possible. "Let's reverse the charm spell so that this town can get back to normal."

Well, somewhat normal for a small town like this one.

If it turned out that the tiny fires breaking out all over town had nothing to do with my mishap of enchanting a magic item, then we still had a mystery to solve. Actually, two.

Where do you keep coming up with this "we" stuff? Do you have a mouse in your pocket?

"Ted, you keep watch. Mom and I will be in the back room reversing the spell." I began walking across the shop, knowing that Leo wouldn't miss this round of free entertainment for all the catnip in the world. "Leo, leave the edibles. We both missed something I did last night with the charm spell, and we can't have anything go wrong this time. Beetle and Wilma will be heading to Vegas by midnight at this current rate."

I'm surprised they aren't already halfway to the airport.

The heart-shaped container that I'd used hadn't been just some trinket. In order for items to be enchanted, they were required to be made of the best materials available, and specifically prepared to accept powerful magic.

It was apparent that Nan had used this item before for some special purpose. She must have labored many hours to construct the glass using her most powerful spells. Why then, had it been laying around the kitchen at the cottage as if it had been another worthless piece of Tupperware or a vase left over from a flower delivery?

"I'm beginning to understand why your grandmother granted Ted life," my mother muttered after I'd passed through the ivory-colored fairy beads that I'd pulled back into place. It wouldn't do to have someone inadvertently see us performing magic. The beads magically provided the barrier we needed to shield us from prying eyes. "Where does he get these more uncommon ingredients?"

I could answer that, but I'm not sure you want to know.

"I find it better not to ask," I replied, meaning every word. Some things were better left a mystery…though not in the case of arson. "Okay. I'm as ready as I'm going to get."

Fine. I won't tell you where Ted gets those ingredients, but don't come crying to me when the police come knocking on your door about his hydroponic grow operation.

It seemed my mother had everything set up on the wooden counter the same way I would have done had I been at home. There was a large pestle and mortar placed in the center of various smaller bowls that held each herb, root, and petal that was needed for the spell. The ancient family grimoire had been propped up against the wall behind my workbench, and Mom had even lit some candles to aid in the flow of energy that we'd need to gather from the earth.

"Wait." There was something missing. "Mom, where's the heart-shaped glass container?"

"Do you really think that I'm that foolish as to touch an enchanted item like that?" My mother crossed her arms and arched her right brow the way she used to do when I was younger and attempting to talk my way out of something. She then wiggled her fingers to let me know that I could retrieve the pink glass vessel myself. "Go."

She doesn't trust your spells, Cupid.

I could see their point, and I definitely didn't have the right to be frustrated. Even so, they didn't have to be so harsh.

Have you ever seen an episode of Abbott and Costello?

"Don't even go there," I warned, slipping back through the beads to fetch the heart-shaped glass container that still held Dee's so-called holistic tea blend that I was scheduled to hand over to her at some point this afternoon. A quick check revealed that Ted was still standing next to the door to keep a lookout, so I hastily made my way back to the storage area. "Okay. Let's do this."

My mother gestured for me to begin with her while Leo monitored every herb, root, and petal I minced together in the pestle. His guidance was constant as always, with measured tones and sound time-honored methods. The grimoire had been turned to the page needed to reverse/dispel an enchantment, so I was finally able to take my place at the center before giving another onceover of the items in front of me.

Everything was perfect.

Briefly closing my eyes allowed me to center my spirit. I let everything around me fade away, though I instantly noticed the intense flowery fragrance wafting from the various copper bowls. There was also a hint of peppermint in the air, but I chalked that up to—

Did you say peppermint?

"Peppermint?" my mother echoed in disbelief. "Tell me you washed out the container before you put the tea leaves inside of it?"

I distinctly remember walking by the counter in the kitchen and thinking Nan had probably gotten the small vessel from one of the quaint shops down past Mindy's boutique. When I spotted the heart-shaped glass gift box sitting on the shelf amongst the other curios Nan had collected—along with literally a ton of other knickknacks—I knew it would be just a perfect touch to Dee's Valentine's Day purchase.

Unfortunately, there had only been one among Nan's collection—for all I knew, the heart-shaped container had probably been once served as a display item containing peppermint candies to catch a shopper's eye.

Oh, it did more than catch your eye. It delivered the town of Paramour Bay into a vast pit of artificial infatuation.

"Technically, even magic can't force someone to fall in love," I argued, not even bothering to try and brush aside my mistake. It was better to own up to my errors, because more were bound to happen with my accident-prone tendencies. "Richard might very well find me attractive, and Candy clearly has a thing for Chief Mason even without her current peppermint-tainted high."

You're forgetting about the mad scientist who's back from the future and now driving around town with a woman who didn't even come from his time.

"Beetle and Wilma?" My mother waved her hand in dismissal. "Infatuation isn't always about true love. Friendship plays a big part in something like this, and Beetle has been doing Wilma's taxes for decades."

"At least now I know what caused the slight hiccup." My

small shrug of regret wasn't going to be good enough. "I'll now forever remember to wash any item I use when casting a spell. Duly noted."

At least now we know why Ted was affected by the spell.

Peppermint was considered many things in the witchcraft world, but one known reflective property was protection. The powdery mint residue must have coated the tea leaves inside the container, thus leaving the outer portion of the glass as a conduit for the spell.

"Trial and error," my mother reassured me in those rare instances she tried her hand at guidance. They'd been few and far between, but I could always count on her in emergencies. "Go on, Raven. Undo the magic so that this town can return to normal."

My evening plans of leisure can subsequently commence!

After a deep calming inhalation, I was able to concentrate on righting the wrong I'd initiated on the contaminated glass container and tea leaves. The verses were spoken, the components minced together, and the energy from the earth utilized to remedy my previous blunder.

I was also able to remove the tea leaves, wipe down the glass with disinfectant, replace the contents with a fresh tea blend, and then cast the original charm spell so that Dee could reconnect with her husband. By the time all was said and done, this day had proven productive...with a few worthwhile lessons tossed in for good measure.

"Mom, I do appreciate you driving all this way to help me."

Could you save the sappiness? I don't need to bear witness to your family curse.

I sincerely meant every word, and I brushed Leo aside so that he had to jump off the counter. Mom hated that I'd chosen to fall into Nan's footsteps, but this was the right path for me. The fact that she was coming around to accepting my decisions was huge.

Don't get me wrong.

It didn't change the fact that Mom had damaged her relationship with Nan out of spite, but hadn't I just learned that mistakes could be fixed with enough determination and desire?

"Raven, you're my daughter." Mom had begun stacking the bowls on top of one another in order to be cleaned later. It was just a way for her to keep busy. She hated when I became emotional, and she always tried to avoid scenes like this one. "I don't always agree with your choices, but I would never allow any harm to come to you if I can prevent it."

Why does that sound more ominous than it should? Has she got anything on her hands?

Leo was right, in a manner of speaking.

My mother was still keeping herself busy by cleaning up the makeshift casting area. I was going to ask her to clarify, especially since the coven in Windsor was about to go to war with one another. Unfortunately, Ted was calling us into the main area of the shop.

Oh, this can't be good.

"Ted?" I was the second one through the ivory-colored fairy beads. Leo had all but poofed into thin air the second the alarm had been rung. "What's wrong?"

"Miss Raven, I think there's been another fire." Ted pointed out toward the glass door with his long, crooked index finger. I followed the direction he was indicating to see the fire truck turning onto Water Way, one of the side streets that led into one of the neighborhoods. "Look. There go Mr. Beetle and Ms. Wilma. Is that Ms. Candy in the backseat?"

Go figure, another clown in the circus car. All we're missing are the elephants and lions.

"Don't jinx us," my mother warned Leo, coming to a stop next to Ted looking out the front window. The two weren't each other's favorite person, but they'd called a ceasefire the last time she was in town. "Your reversal of the charm spell apparently didn't stop what was sparking these fires."

Don't say it, Raven.

"Leo, you can't stop a determined criminal," I warned, not surprised when Liam walked out of the police station. He stopped long enough to give me a wave before hopping into his truck and driving off…in the exact direction of the fire truck. "Paramour Bay has an arsonist in its midst."

Chapter Seven

"RAVEN, THAT SMOKE isn't coming from the residential addition. It looks like it's coming from somewhere over on Oceanview, near the treasurer's office, maybe."

My mother and I had just stepped out onto the sidewalk when she gestured toward a plume of black smoke billowing up into the overcast sky. We'd already decided to grab a bite to eat at the diner, where I had every intention of discreetly discussing spells that could potentially give me some insight into who was responsible for the outbreak of these troublesome fires. It was going on three o'clock in the afternoon, late enough to miss the tail end of the lunch mob and early enough to avoid the dinner crowd. We were relatively guaranteed a booth of our choice in the back.

"That's odd," I murmured, briefly concentrating on locking up the shop. Ted had gone over to Mindy's boutique to stare through the window display, and Leo was in seventh heaven with a pouch of fresh tuna I'd brought from home. There wouldn't be morsel left by the time I got back. I was hoping he wouldn't eat the packaging, too. "Unless Chief Mason was just using Water Way Avenue as a shortcut. Creek Bed Road parallels River Bay."

"That's right," my mother murmured, probably recalling the streets from when she was younger. "There's also a fire hydrant on the corner of Creek Bed and Oceanview. We used to pop one of the valves halfway open and dance in the spray on hot days."

We strolled over to the intersection, where it was easy to see a few of the townsfolk gathered on the sidewalk down yonder.

"Are you absolutely positive that the original charm spell couldn't have caused this mayhem?" I believed in coincidences, but categorizing today's activities as one might be wishful thinking. "Mom, maybe we should—"

"Raven, you have nothing to worry about. Charm spells don't release fire elementals or summon sprites with a match fetish, even if you'd added an ingredient or two." My mother crossed the intersection without hesitation. "Let your sheriff handle these fires, and give poor Leo a break. He's had a tough day. At this rate, all of his hair is going to fall out."

I had no choice but to fall into step with her, giving a small wave to Newt. The mechanic was test driving Otis' vehicle, most likely trying to detect the source of the mysterious squeak that the older gentleman swore had been there for the past month. Not even his wife could hear it amongst the other engine noises, but Otis was unwavering in his quest to prove he was right. He was bound and determined to find out the exact cause.

"Don't let Leo fool you," I replied, continuing our conversation. We'd made it safely to the other side of the street, although I certainly had to skedaddle to keep up with her pace. I didn't understand why she was in such a hurry all of a sudden. "He actually enjoys solving these little mysteries that pop up every now and then."

"Your version of the saying *every now and then* versus mine is vastly different," my mother replied wryly, passing the police station without a second glance. I couldn't do that and made sure to wave to Eileen who was sitting at her desk just inside the office. "No one says you have to live up to your reputation on the other side. Your grandmother just wanted you to be happy with the tea shop and her little side business bilking the natives out of their Social Security money."

What my mother meant by reputation was the fact that Leo and I had been sought out by a tea-drinking ghost—yes, a real dead apparition—last month to determine why her familiar didn't cross through the veil with her.

Remember that fairy kiss that wouldn't come off of Leo's paw?

Well, let's just say that Mazie Rose Young and her fairy familiar were quite the handful.

Anyway, Mazie had made mention of the fact that Leo and I were known on the other side as promising amateur sleuths, something that had stuck with me ever since her visit.

There were a lot of mysteries to solve that involved the supernatural that Liam or other humans couldn't solve, because they didn't understand the occult. If Leo and I could help in any way, shouldn't we at least try like any other good citizen would do?

As for the Social Security quip...well, that was just below the belt. Nan wasn't here to speak for herself, but I certainly didn't create those magical tea blends to bilk anyone out of their hard-earned money. Some of these residents had ailments that couldn't be cured by modern medicine.

"I know it's in the middle of the afternoon, but Heidi has been raving about Trixie's pancakes." It didn't surprise me when my mother couldn't leave well enough alone. She was able to get one snide remark in before opening the door to the diner. "I don't remember them being anything spectacular, but we'll see if I change my mind."

The delicious smell of coffee was the first thing that washed over me after entering the diner. The cold from outside quickly vacated as my favorite beverage left my mouth watering. I'd have to get my mother to order a cup and sneak sips on the side, because it wouldn't do for me to be seen drinking anything other than the tea. On top of that, I provided this establishment its tea assortment from my business.

I really, really needed to begin the initiative to add gourmet coffee blends to my inventory. A nice Columbian Supremo would be fantastic right now. Dark and rich, fresh out of a French press.

"Has Heidi ever steered you wrong?" I replied in an attempt to lighten the mood and take my mind off the coffee fantasy that had definitely distracted me. Remember, my mother wasn't the biggest fan of Paramour Bay. She'd up and left the town thirty years ago, but a lot had changed—including my mother. "Trixie still serves breakfast all day, so I'm sure you can try them out if you promise to keep your opinions to yourself."

Like I said before, it was going on three o'clock in the afternoon. The lunch hour rush had cleared out, and it was a little too early for the dinner crowd to be leaving work. With that said, there were only a few tables and booths that had been previously claimed. I was a bit surprised to find that Billy and his parents were sitting at one of the tables.

Pete and Sarah Owen didn't look as upset as I would have thought, but maybe that was because Billy had cleared up this misunderstanding and cleared his name. He wasn't at fault for the fires. Unfortunately, that still left an arsonist on the loose with no clues as to his identity.

"My heavens, are we truly being graced by the presence of Regina Lattice Marigold?"

Ugh. This was so not the way to settle my mother down in the diner for a quiet meal before she drove back to the city.

What was Trixie thinking in goading Mom like that?

"Why did we come here again?" my mother murmured, pasting a smile on her face that said whatever patience she had before arriving into town had now thinned to the point of snapping like a twig. "Trixie, it's good to see you looking so healthy."

That was a dig if I ever heard one, but at least my mother made an effort, right?

"What brings you into town on a workday?" Trixie was quite a lot older than my mother, but at least she didn't have to rely on a cane yet. She waved the hostess away and gathered up two menus before following us to the back booth. As I'd predicted, no one had claimed either one at this time of day. "Did you hear about those fires? I was just talking with the Owens about who might be setting them. Poor Billy was seen cutting through the alleyway, but Liam got things straightened out before Monty could start pointing any fingers."

I'd heard that Billy hadn't always been so innocent, going so far as to swipe the candy out of the container that Monty kept for the children of his customers. Eugene and Albert—the two elderly men who played chess over at the shop—were better than any alarm system Monty could ever invest in, and they'd seen Billy's grubby little fingers grab a handful of wrapped bubblegum out of the dish.

Granted, that had been several years ago, but these old folks had memories like steel traps with rusty hinges. Once someone earned a reputation with those old geezers, even a life prison sentence wouldn't serve as payment enough to redeem your name.

"Monty never did like Billy after that," Pete Owen said with a frown, making his opinion known. It wasn't like the Owen family couldn't hear Trixie give a recount of today's events. "Liam went down to the hardware store to straighten things out. It does seem like we have a spree arsonist on our hands, though. First your tea shop, then Monty's hardware store. The next fire was out at Beetle's house."

"I heard that the pub had a small fire inside, but that turned out to be a false alarm," Alice Abbott chimed in over her cup of tea. At least someone was drinking tea today. Trixie always made sure to put in a monthly order of English Breakfast and Earl Grey for her clientele. "What is this world coming to?"

While Trixie and Alice began debating the decline of society in general, I had taken the side of the booth that afforded me the luxury of seeing every table and booth in the diner. I noticed right away that Billy hadn't looked up from his plate. He was purposefully staying out of the conversation, but I don't believe it was out of guilt.

With that said, I couldn't pinpoint exactly what he might be trying to hide.

"I'll have the pancakes and link sausage, please," my mother ordered after having hung up her dress coat on the small silver hook attached to each booth. I had sat down in mine, but I did unbutton it and push it down off my shoulders behind me. I didn't miss the glare Mom gave me in disapproval, but I'd had one heck of a day and the vinyl seats were always so cold against my legs. Anyway, I was allowed to be lazy when I wanted to be. "With a cup of coffee and a small orange juice, please."

I'd already resigned myself to the fact that I wasn't going to get a sip of that coffee.

You know what?

Every person had a breaking point, and I'd reached mine today.

"Trixie, I'll have the same," I announced loudly, secretly waiting for the ceiling to collapse right on top of me. When nothing happened, I'd noticed that Trixie was still waiting for me to switch that coffee to tea. "I want to try your coffee this time around. I was thinking of incorporating some high-end coffee blends, but I'm not sure where to start with my inventory. I always like to dive head first into my research."

"Coffee?" Alice tilted her head slightly as if she weren't sure she'd heard me correctly. "Well, I guess it wouldn't be so bad to have a variety of ingredients for the two most popular hot beverages in your store to widen your potential customer base. My Bob has one of those machines that brews him one cup at a time. It saves money, because I drink my tea. That way, he doesn't have to brew an entire pot just for himself."

"I second that idea," Pete Owen said, lifting a hand so that I would know I could count on him as a customer. Relief ran rampant through my body, and I couldn't wait to share the news with Liam. Although I would be a bit sad that he no longer had to sneak me coffee throughout the day. That had been our special little secret only the two of us shared. "We're a coffee family, so it would be nice to have somewhere local to get our premium caffeine fix."

My dream of turning the tea shop into a small hot beverage café might actually work, but I'd still take baby steps to get there. At the rate things were burning down around here, there wouldn't be a main thoroughfare to shop on.

Trixie had already left our table to let the chef know our order, plus to hand off the drink orders to Paula. She was new in town, but Trixie mentioned knowing her from somewhere. It was the reason everyone accepted the younger woman so easily, though I didn't recall hearing the story of how the two of them met.

"Have you studied the book in more detail?" my mother asked me quietly so that no one could overhear our conversation. She was still careful in what she said, but I got the reference to the family's grimoire. "There are short cantrips in the back that can benefit you in times like these."

"Are you talking about the one for the Freudian Slip?" I whispered, leaning over the table. Everyone had gone back to eating anyway. "I thought those types of quick offensive tricks required stored physical energy…a power source."

Regina Lattice Marigold did all she could not to reach across the table and strangle me. Her frustration was obvious, but I'd thought my question was reasonable.

"What?" I gave a small shrug, having looked through the family grimoire a thousand times over the last four months. "I'm telling you, all those truth spells require ingredients."

"I'm not talking about those in the main body," my mother muttered in irritation. It was a good thing Leo wasn't around to hear this conversation. "I'm referring to the aura divinations known as cantrips. They don't need anything more than a vocal component."

"You mean the ones that show the person's color?" I asked in surprise, fully believing that topic had been thoroughly debunked. "Haven't you been keeping up with your horoscope? I read online somewhere that a person's aura closely matches their zodiac sign. Billy turned eighteen back in September, so he's a Virgo. His aura should be royal blue. That's not going to help me figure out if he had anything to do with those fires."

"You always were a difficult child to teach," my mother

muttered, somehow knowing that Paula was heading our way with a tray in her hand. Mom leaned back and stopped our conversation. "Hand me the sugar, please."

I slid the small rectangular holder that contained several kinds of sweeteners with both artificial substitutes and the real McCoy toward her, but I made sure to smile a welcoming greeting at our waitress.

"Paula, we haven't officially met." It was my turn to lean back in my seat so that Paula could set down the two cups of coffee onto the table. "I'm Raven Marigold, and this is my mother—Regina. I own the tea shop across the street. It's nice to meet you."

The younger woman was in her mid-twenties, and I'd heard through Elsie and Wilma that she was renting the room above the local pub. I couldn't imagine how loud the small apartment was in the evening, what with it being above a bar and all. From the way Paula was smiling, it didn't seem to keep her up at night.

"It's nice to meet you, too. Everyone in this town is so nice, it reminds me of the café back home." Paula also set down two small containers of creamer, one for Mom and one for me. "Your meals should be ready in around five minutes. If you need anything else, please just give me a holler."

I'd wanted to ask Paula where home was, but she'd left the table before I could get the words out.

"West Virginia."

"West Virginia…what?"

Mom was being rather vague again, but that was par for the course.

"Your new waitress is from a small town in West Virginia," Regina revealed, tearing open two pink packets and pouring the artificial additives into her coffee. I grimaced and stuck with the real stuff intended for us to use…not a packet full of chemicals. "Now, back to this garbage you've been reading on the internet. Raven, that family book you have in your possession wasn't carefully put together for the sake of being disproven by some idiot with nothing better to do with their time than make up stories while living in their parent's basement."

Mom carefully poured the creamer into her coffee before leisurely stirring the contents as if she had all the time in the world. I almost asked if she were going to spend the night, but I'd wait for that bad news after I finally put something in my stomach.

"Do you remember any of the aura cantrips?" Mom asked, tapping her spoon on the rim of the coffee cup. I was so happy to do the same that I almost didn't respond. I was too busy swirling the hot, rich flavor around on my tongue. There was nothing more satisfying than that first sip of creamy coffee. "Raven, pay attention."

"Yes, I remember the first two from the back cover." I quickly took another sip in case my mother made it impossible to enjoy the rest of my drink with whatever she had in mind. "There were only three verses in the one, and four verses in the second."

"They technically do the same thing, but try the first one," Mom recommended, never taking her eyes off me. She was really good at this spy stuff. "Pretend you're stirring more cream into your coffee. Go ahead. The simple somatic movement, along with the verbal components, will generate the energy you need to cast the cantrip."

It was times like these that I got a sneaking suspicion that my mother never really gave up anything after leaving Paramour Bay to start a new life. Maybe she just didn't want to have magic in her daily life, the way Nan had. Or, maybe she didn't want the restrictions of an overbearing mother standing over her while she wove her story.

Regina Lattice Marigold was one of those secretive type women who would take things to their grave…I guess she was following in my grandmother's footsteps.

"Stop squirreling around and concentrate," Mom ordered, lifting the coffee cup to her red painted lips. I was flabbergasted that she understood what squirreling meant, but the arch of her brow told me that she was losing her patience. "Proceed."

Fine. If she wanted me to prove her wrong about these auras, then I would.

I poured a little more creamer into my coffee—not enough to mess with the taste, though—and proceeded to stir the contents with my spoon. I stared inside the cup, becoming mesmerized by the continuous motion. It wasn't hard to conjure up the energy, which I'd been finding easier and easier to draw lately.

The spoon was serving as my conduit, so I didn't waste time in reciting the short verses.

Show yourself to me.
Reveal yourself to thee.
The color is key.
Show yourself to me.

I had read up on horoscope and astrology a long time ago, and I recalled the colors of specific months. Of course, my aura should have been indigo. I had been born on Halloween, which meant I was a Scorpio. Seeing as I was still staring at my cup of coffee, you can imagine my surprise when a bright green hue radiated from my body.

Drat.

I've gone and messed up again.

The incantation had been meant for Billy, but I'd done it to myself instead. I quickly glanced up, hoping that no one else was witnessing my blunder, only to find my mother's red lips raised in the right corner with satisfaction.

Ohhhhh....

All around her emanated a reddish-orange. I recall that color signified confidence and that she was a force to be reckoned with.

Well, wasn't that the unadulterated truth?

My gaze finally slid away from her and toward the intended target. He was finishing off his sandwich and plopping a fry in his mouth as if he hadn't just spent the last hour at the police station defending his honor.

"What do you see?" my mother asked softly, indicating that only I could see the aura of every individual inside the diner. "Is there a blackness swirling inside his aura?"

No, but amazingly, his aura was indigo. He was an introvert, keeping to himself with the exception of those he truly trusted. There wasn't an ounce of black churning inside the beautiful hue he was generating.

"There's your answer, Raven. Billy Owen is not your culprit."

No, he wasn't. But the arsonist might very well be inside his family.

"Raven?"

"Mom, Pete Owen has streaks of black running through his aura," I whispered, taken aback by the startling sight. "Could Billy's father be the arsonist?"

Chapter Eight

W*HAT WAS YOUR mother thinking? Dear Angel of Mercy, strike me down swiftly.*

"We don't have to keep rehashing yesterday's events," I grumbled, having heard the near continuous lecture that witchcraft shouldn't be used as a method for invasion of privacy. By the time Leo got done reaming us both out, I was pretty sure that particular aura spell should be burned. "Mom was just trying to help us narrow down the suspect pool."

I bought myself a little time from hearing another sermon by flipping the sign on the door to signify we were open. Leo and I usually liked to quietly watch the town come alive as each of the shops' lights came on one by one, but I had a feeling that wouldn't be happening today.

Leo was pacing in the display window, telling me that our daily ritual was about to be nixed on account of my slow learning curve. At his current rate of pacing, I'd have to repaint the wooden surface of the windowsill by this afternoon.

He was so amped up over yesterday's debacle, I had to wonder if he got any sleep last night.

You randomly peered into everyone's soul, Raven! You invited yourself to witness their most fundamental vulnerabilities without their consent! You took from them without their permission, which makes you no better than a thief!

"How is that any different than pulling up the memory of the victim or the guilty party of a crime, as we've done in the past?" I'd been wanting to ask that question since yesterday, but things had gone from bad to worse when a couple of businesses located on Oceanview had gone up in smoke. I sipped the all-too-limited supply of coffee hidden inside my tea cup while trying to see if there was still smoke rising in the air. "We've done that particular incantation several times, Leo."

Leo finally plopped on his haunches with an uncontrollable tic to his bulging left eye. The learning curve to this witchcraft stuff was really, really steep. He needed to cut me a break, and the long audible sigh that twitched his whiskers told me he'd finally run out of steam.

How do I put this so you'll understand?

Leo's tail thwacked the hardwood of the bench seat inside the display window as he contemplated his analogy. He was always big on using comparisons to explain the suitability of a spell, so it wasn't surprising that he would do so in this situation.

You're wearing clothes. Right? You don't mind when people stare at you.

Well, I wasn't going to say that a stranger—man or woman—staring at me for no reason wasn't awkward. Of course, it was.

Either way, Leo had pointed out the obvious.

I glanced down at my peacock skirt with different shades of burgundies and greens blended together. I had a ton of these in my closet consisting of different colors, but this one was my favorite. I'd really needed the pick-me-up today.

Now imagine if I had a pair of x-ray vision glasses and they allowed me to see through those clothes. Would it be fair of me to randomly look at anyone I cared to undress? Or maybe I should allow others to rent them, and do the same to whomever they want to perv out on?

Hmphf. When Leo put it like, I could see where he was coming from.

A person's memories are like a collection of items—stamps, coins, you get the drift. Summoning up those memories to help solve a mystery are like discovering clues. Have you ever seen a police lineup on television where all those men and women holding numbers are laid bare? No—no, you do not. Everyone has a certain expectation of privacy that shouldn't be violated without a valid moral reason based on due process of law or in our exparte case—where we can't be heard aloud in the court of human opinion. We need a darn good reason to look, one in which we've weighed against their expectations and found it is in the best interest of the common good. Bottom line? You need a moral reason to look.

"Leo, I have to hand it to you…that was very well explained." I made my way over to the cash register, feeling lower than dirt. It hit me that the divination shouldn't even be used except in rare instances, yet my mother had no qualms about using such a spell to randomly pry. "Why did Nan include something like that in the family grimoire to begin with? I mean, we can't be the only ones to have that type of easily accessible magic."

Those types of divinations should only be used in the direst of circumstances—like life and death situations. Your mother should have known better, but she avoided her formal training and has suffered as a result.

I'm pretty sure Mom had just wanted to show me that witchcraft could be used in many different ways and in many different circumstances. With that said, she did allow me to utilize a wing-dinger of a spell and it hadn't even required massive preparation of power.

"We're not facing an apocalypse as of yet, but Pete Owen isn't the most upstanding citizen according to the nature of his aura," I pointed out, still trying to figure out a way to let Liam know that Billy's father might be the one responsible for the fires or some other criminal intent. I shouldn't have used the spell yesterday, but it had been cast nonetheless. Now I had indirect information that could play a part in stopping these arsons and return Paramour Bay to normal. "I somehow need to let Liam know that Mr. Owen is a prime suspect to be investigated."

Have you not heard a word I said? Just because you saw streaks of black on his aura does not mean that good old Petey is setting fires around town. The man is in his forties, and I'm sure he's done a thing or two in his past that he feels regret for, and therefore carries a certain amount of guilt. If the blackness had been threatening to take over the brightness of his other hue, that's when we'd have a problem that I'd gladly turn over to your mother. No sense in all of us sacrificing ourselves on the altar for the greater good.

One good thing came of this morning's conversation, and that was the fact that Leo had calmed down a bit. Let's just say that my mother ended up driving back to the city last night after she and Leo had traded broadsides, low blows, and insults...but thankfully nothing so bad that had them resorting to spell combat to vanquish one another.

On that silver lining, Wilma and Beetle's admiration for one another had dimmed somewhat to their former friendship. I hadn't seen hide nor hair of Richard, and my little charm mishap might have actually resulted in a newfound relationship. Word around town had it that Chief Mason asked Candy out for dinner, and she happily accepted regardless of the fact that her hair made her head look like an Easter egg.

There was only one thing left unresolved.

Can't you for once let the good ol' sheriff do his job on his own?

"We're helping like we always do. There's a difference. And if you don't believe that Pete Owen's guilt is a result of setting those fires, then it looks like we're back to square one," I said, walking around the counter so that I could pull out my laptop. Thursday mornings were always a tad bit slow, but it was a welcome relief compared to the chaos of yesterday. "There should be an online map of Paramour Bay that can give us a better view of the town. Maybe the fires weren't random, after all."

Oh, thank the supernatural! My supply of edibles has arrived, and just in in time.

"Good morning, my dear Raven," Beetle greeted as he came barreling into the shop. His entrances were like that of a hurricane, but his energy was quite infectious. Although, that might have been the coffee talking. "I'm sorry to say that I won't be able to have one of our training sessions this morning. Sorry, indeed. I have business elsewhere today."

Where are my edibles? I'd like to report that this employee has failed in his most sacred of duties. Raven, I'm afraid he needs to be let go.

I stared at Beetle in horror as the realization of why he couldn't work today hit me like an energy ball. Oh, this was bad. Really, really bad.

I agree. No catnip is bad. Does this man not realize the week I've had?

"Beetle, was one of the offices that burnt down yesterday yours?" I asked, coming back around the counter to meet him halfway. "No one said a word to me, other than the fact that Chief Mason thought the fire had started in the treasurer's office."

Are you trying to break it to me gently that all of my edibles have been burned alive? The horror of it all. We need to find this villain, pronto!

"Oliver is mighty upset," Beetle exclaimed, rubbing his hand over his chin as he contemplated his own predicament. "Mighty upset, and I don't blame him. I'm going to be spending the rest of the week attempting to get my clients to reprint all of their receipts and any paperwork that went along with them. What a mess. A complete mess, I tell you."

Would this be a bad time to ask Beetle exactly how much catnip he had stored in his office?

"At least most of your clients are local," I pointed out, wishing there was something I could do to help Beetle with the amount of work he had cut out for him. "Insurance should cover the damage to the office, and I can go around at lunchtime asking the other shop owners to duplicate their tax receipts and anything else applicable to their year-end finances. I do insist that they keep all originals for reasons of an audit or something of this very nature."

Insurance? Oh, that's great news! Any catnip he had stashed will be covered!

When I'd first moved to Paramour Bay, it was a given that Heidi would complete the tea shop's taxes. It had never even crossed my mind to keep things status quo, especially considering that Heidi was my best friend. Maybe she would have some suggestions to help Beetle in his time of need, especially considering she was very interested in buying out his business.

Heidi can fix anything. Hey, let's give her a call now!

"It wouldn't be so bad if my computer hadn't caught fire." Beetle shook his head in misery, and I didn't blame him. All that work he'd put into his clients' taxes had been destroyed with the simple strike of a match. "I'll have to start from scratch and recover my backup files to rebuild everything on a new machine."

Raven, do something. I can't stand to see this poor man suffer.

"Beetle, let me make a phone call." There was a slim chance that Heidi knew of a computer whiz who could recover data from a burnt hard drive. "And why don't you write down the name of some of your clients so that I can pay them a visit during the lunch hour today?"

"My dear Raven, you are an absolute saint to want to help me," Beetle gushed, patting his cardigan sweater and somehow finding a pen that must have been tucked away in the pocket of his dress shirt underneath. "A saint, I tell you!"

Not to burst your bubble, but Beetle wouldn't be saying such a thing if the reason he lost his life's work had been due to your attempt of a charm spell.

"I take it that Leo's catnip you sneak him every day got burnt to a crisp?" I asked before reaching into my pocket for my cell phone.

Touché.

I sent Leo a satisfied smile that let him know two could play his game. I also had a sense of inspiration that I was able to help those in need, which we should all do more often. Although Oliver Bend wasn't my most favorite person, I'd still give him a call to see if there was anything I could do to help. That was the benefit to living in a small town.

"Oh, no," Beetle replied to my question after having written down some shops that I could visit later this morning. "No, no. The premium catnip I buy for him came to the house. That way, I never forget to slip a small packet in my breast pocket every morning. Ta-da!"

You know that saying *his eyes lit up with happiness*? That was the only way to describe the expression of euphoria on Leo's furry face when Beetle pulled out a tiny package of catnip from underneath his cardigan sweater.

I love this man, Raven. Just love him. In his hour of need, he remembers those he loves.

Leo had adopted Beetle's habit of repeating phrases, but I'd let him have this moment of bliss. He'd find out soon enough that I planned to use the upcoming visits to the various shops to snoop around to see who had access to all the places that had been set on fire.

Our first arson investigation could now commence unabated by my familiar.

Chapter Nine

THIS IS REALLY a bad idea.

"You're always saying the sky is falling," I complained, tucking my scarf into my dress coat to keep the cold wind from sneaking under my lapel. All that was left to do was grab my keys and purse from behind the cash register. "This is the perfect opportunity to do a little digging."

Maybe for a doomsday bunker. There is usually no digging required as a witch, just in case you missed that in your nightly reading assignment...which you never seem to get around to.

The morning had passed by relatively quickly, though not without progress. I'd actually checked a lot off my own list of things to do.

The research into the coffee blends had gone way better than I'd expected. There were literally hundreds of gourmet coffee blends available from wholesale coffee outlets. One of the vendors had been having a sale, so I placed a small five-pound order of fifteen different coffee blends. I also chose a popular brand of French presses to stock, as well. I wasn't sure how well those would go over, so I also had to purchase some single cup machines and the reusable copperware pods that came with them for those who didn't want the hassle of making an entire pot of coffee.

Me?

I'd perfected my French press technique, adored the drip coffee makers, and would use the single cup makers when I needed a quick fix while on the run.

You make a good point, and it's come full circle. Are you ready for this? You need to look at my catnip addiction like your coffee dependence. See? We'd all be happier. Ted needs to add raising hydroponic catnip to his garden of spell components.

Another thing I'd been able to do was place a call into Heidi, who swore she had a super geek technical wizard on staff at her current place of business. She'd even mentioned that she'd already had a talk with her employer about leaving at the end of tax season to take over Beetle's firm. Apparently, he'd handled it well, though that might have had something to do with Heidi expressing that she'd love to have some sort of partnership for those times when her clients needed more than what she alone could offer in the way of services.

Heidi also mentioned that the deal she'd proposed included technical support on select occasions to ensure their software programs were compatible. There was no time like the present to review what changes would need to be made by rebuilding Beetle's current systems and securing that information at a third party redundant offsite data management service.

Heidi's boss, of course, had been very receptive to her idea—more business, more money. Seeing as the fire had technically affected her future, he'd given her the first half of next week off to get things reconstituted with aforementioned technical support in very short order.

It was really happening.

My best friend was moving to Paramour Bay. Contracts and NDAs would be signed...and then it would be set in stone.

And I'd like for us to still be alive for when that eventual cause for celebration happens. Can we get back to the genesis of this bad idea of yours?

"Leo, it's not like I'm going to stand in the middle of the street and shout that we're looking for an arsonist. We're not playing a game of kick the can, and I'm not calling ollie, ollie, oxen free." I slipped on my gloves, grabbed my keys and purse, and then snatched up the list Beetle had left behind. Even with Heidi claiming her whiz kid could retrieve Beetle's computer files, Beetle would still need all the receipts and paperwork from those accounts he hadn't been able to work on this month. "I have a little more decorum than that. I'm just going to tag someone and say they're it."

This comic relief is coming from the witch who tossed an energy ball at a known killer in one of the bedrooms at the Paramour Bay Inn with a state police detective only two rooms away. Can you work out why I'm not laughing?

"Leo, we have a chance here to do some investigating without anyone being the wiser." I held up the list as I walked toward the door. "I'd like this mystery solved before tomorrow evening's dinner with Liam."

It all seems to come back to the good ol' sheriff.

"Leave Liam alone," I warned, not putting it past Leo to do something that would foil my dinner plans. He'd made it quite well known that he believed my relationship with Liam was a mistake from the word go. He had a point, but not in the way you think. I hadn't been able to keep my secret from Heidi, so I could understand why Leo would have trouble believing I'd be able to keep from blurting out that I was a witch over a candlelit dinner. "I've handled things quite well thus far, haven't I?"

I didn't wait for Leo to answer my question, but instead opened the door and stepped out onto the sidewalk. The temperatures were hovering in the high forties or lower fifties, so the bite from the wind gusts weren't as ferocious as they had been. With that said, I was still glad I'd tucked my scarf in tight and put on my faux fur-lined imitation leather gloves.

I'd stay behind and roll in that huge bag of catnip Beetle left behind, but I'm afraid to leave you alone on this little quest of yours.

"I knew you'd come around to my way of thinking," I muttered underneath my breath, just in case anyone was watching me. The colder temps kept the window shoppers to a minimum, but it also gave the shop owners the downtime to spy on one another from their perches. "Is Eileen still looking out the window?"

Her glittery snowflake enhanced sweater is hard to miss. It's a wonder we all don't suffer from migraines while looking at her. She might actually be a gorgon.

"First up, the malt shop."

You keep whoever is working busy while I look for the matches and a flamethrower.

No one had said a thing about flamethrowers, or matches for that matter, but I got Leo's gist. He'd look for anything suspicious while I talked to the shop owner. I almost mentioned that his snooping was just as bad as my canvassing the diner's patrons with an aura spell, but then thought of the clothing analogy he'd come up with. A quick peek around a public shop wasn't too bad in the morality department, right?

I'm sure Dr. Jekyll believes it's a little late for the morality police, Mrs. Hyde, don't you agree?

Considering that the bell above the malt shop door chimed at my entrance, I'd say Leo was right on the money. I wouldn't have stopped this investigation, no matter the consequences. I really was looking forward to my dinner with Liam tomorrow night, and we deserved a wonderful Valentine's Day free of murder and mayhem.

This was going to sound rather sappy, but I'd never had the best Valentine's Day. Usually, Heidi and I ended up eating a box of chocolates and watching *Love, Actually* while drowning our sorrows in a bucket of wine.

Pitiful. Just pitiful, corrupting that poor girl.

"Hi, Miss Marigold," Sam greeted with a sweet smile. I'd seen him put away his phone right as I walked across the threshold, but I couldn't say anything considering I sometimes browsed on mine when the shop was quiet. "What can I get you today? Another chocolate malt?"

"I was hoping to speak with Cora." I was quite surprised to see Otis and his wife enjoying an afternoon shake at one of the tables. I'd have to say hello before I left, but business came first. "Is she around?"

"No, but I can get Bonnie for you." Sam didn't give me a chance to tell him that it wasn't necessary that I speak with anyone else, but he'd already shouted out the manager's name. "She'll be right out, I'm sure."

I'm pleasantly surprised by how clean these floors are back here. Young Sammy does good work.

It appeared that Leo had made his way around the counter. The only problem with having Leo around other people while he was invisible was the chance we took that his short-term memory might kick in and he forgot where he was at or why he was here.

I'm not sure if you've noticed or not, but catnip does help in that department. I haven't had an episode in quite some time.

I was pretty sure that Leo had made that part up, but it was a little late to change our plans at this late stage.

"Hi, Miss Marigold." Bonnie had come out of the back

room that no doubt held a small office. Cora Barnes was nothing if not efficient. "What can I do for you?"

You're right about Cora. It's really nice back here. This leather chair is plush and...yeah, my claws go right through it like butter. It's way better than any scratching post I've ever owned.

It took all of my reserve not to go running around the ice cream counter and yank Leo off the leather chair.

This is certainly better than that scratching post you bought me for Christmas.

"I was just looking for Cora," I explained with a pasted smile on my lips. Had I pulled off am unconcerned air? I wasn't so sure when Bonnie tilted her head to the side in question. "I'm not sure you know, but Beetle's office was one of the locations hit by the fires that have been being set around town. He was hoping that Cora or Desmond could reprint off copies of their financial files and their receipts for the past tax year so that he could get a jump on redoing their taxes."

What's that?

Leo's commentary from the other room was setting me on edge. It was a bad idea to have him come with me on this little quest.

"Mr. Barnes is out of town," Sam offered up with a regretful shrug. "You might be able to find Cora over at the hair salon. She has a standard afternoon appointment with Candy every Wednesday."

Yuck. It's a piece of chewed gum stuck underneath the desk. I bet it was Sam's doing. I'm done back here. This place is clear. No arsonist handbooks lying about turned to the page on burning down Rome.

Bonnie nodded her agreement about Cora's whereabouts, but I didn't speak fast enough to cover up the small crash that came from the back room. The petite blonde turned and it was clear she was going to go investigate what had caused the sound.

Oops. I knocked over a copy of the Anarchist Cookbook. My bad. Ohhhh, there is a book on Cancun. As much as I love the sunshine, those scaly lizards will keep me away from paradise. Those suckers are bigger than me.

"Bonnie, do you think you could tell Cora about the financial forms and tax receipts? It would be great if you could relay my message," I continued, rattling off whatever thoughts came to mind in order to give Leo time to vacate. Granted, Bonnie wouldn't be able to see Leo if he remained invisible, but I wasn't going to take that chance. "As a matter of fact, why don't you give me a piece of paper? I'll write down a list of what Beetle needs for the malt shop's year end."

Back to this other book, did you know that you can make napalm in your own bathroom? No, thanks. I like my weapons of mass destruction kept in the garage.

"I can give the list to Roger," Bonnie offered, reaching for a small pad and pencil next to the cash register. She slid them over to me while she explained her reasoning. "Roger has been here a lot longer than I have, and he's the one who closes out our receipts every night and makes the bank drop. He's just been out sick for the last couple of days. Cora usually has him compile the receipts and financial information in a binder for Beetle. I'm sure he keeps copies for himself and Cora."

No cigarettes, no matches, and no gasoline. You can put a checkmark on your list next to the malt shop.

I wrote down basically what I'd already said to Sam and Bonnie, but it gave me something to do while I figured out how to ask the next question without blatantly revealing the real reason for my visit.

I already told you the coast was clear. On to the next shop. And did you ever think that maybe one of the firemen staged these fires to have something to do? I saw a movie with a similar plot line, you know.

"I appreciate you passing this onto Roger and Cora." I set the pencil down on the pad and then focused on Sam. It was proper to ask about yesterday's events, right? Leo's theory about firemen going rogue didn't add up. "How is Billy doing after yesterday's dose of excitement? I saw him and his parents at the diner after they were through speaking with Liam. Billy seemed relieved."

Liam wasn't one to go by his official title, and the town was rather informal like that.

Why are you so focused on Billy? You already know that he's innocent.

"Billy explained why he was here and the reason he used the back alleyway of Monty's hardware shop to get home." Sam shrugged as if it had been no big deal. "There haven't been any more fires. Bonnie and I were just saying that Liam should check with the school to see who else didn't show up for class yesterday. It had to have been a teenager running around town."

All I could focus on was that Sam had pointed out there hadn't been any more fires since yesterday. What if the last fire *had* been set before I'd reversed the charm spell? What if the reason so much damage had been done was due to the fact the fire hadn't been called in right away?

Nice detective work, Sherlock. Can we stop this goose chase now? It seems as if you've found your culprit—yourself. You set the town on fire with your own version of fiery passion.

Chapter Ten

I SPENT THE rest of my lunch break hitting nearly every shop in town, letting those who used Beetle's tax services know that they would have to reprint copies of their financials. It had taken over an hour, especially because Gertie had invited me inside the inn for a cup of tea. I, in turn, advised her of my incoming inventory of gourmet coffees.

Honestly, coffee was what I needed most after discovering that the likelihood I may have been responsible for the fires yesterday was becoming very real.

Leo had abandoned me early on, claiming to be in need of an emergency nap. It wasn't a surprised to find him asleep in his bed inside the display window. He was splayed out, sleeping deeply when I arrived.

He wasn't the type to curl up in a ball the way most cats do when sleeping. No, Leo was on his back with his mouth open, tongue hanging out, and paws stretched out so that his belly got every ounce of toasty sunshine it could possibly get from the ten seconds it had shown itself so far today.

I let him continue to sleep as I went about my business, walking into the back room to hang up my dress coat. I debated calling my mother, but I didn't want to rehash what happened yesterday and Leo's issue with the morality of it all. The belief that my failed spell was responsible for so much damage—and a potential life-threatening crime—was incomprehensible. I could only console myself by realizing that no one had been hurt.

It was best to forget the chaos caused by a spell gone bad and focus on the future.

The bell above the door chimed right as I'd come back through the ivory-colored fairy beads. Now that was a sight to lift my spirits, and I wasn't talking about the coffee in Liam's hands.

"I tried to stop in earlier, but the shop was closed," Liam said as he came closer. I still couldn't get over the way the brown suede jacket formed across his wide shoulders just so. He sure was a sight for sore eyes…and a bruised ego. "Everything okay?"

"I went around town helping Beetle ask his clients to reprint all of their statements and receipts so that he could spend the morning seeing what was salvageable from the office." I gratefully took the cup from his hands, but I wasn't prepared for when he leaned in close. He searched my gaze for something I couldn't name right before his warm lips brushed against mine. I could definitely get used to this kind of attention. "Well, that warmed me up."

"Glad I could help," Liam murmured, pulling back and taking his precious source of heat with him. It was nice to see him a bit more relaxed than yesterday, which once again confirmed my suspicion that I *had* been responsible for the fires. "The town has been relatively quiet since Oliver and Beetle lost their offices. I did, however, spend the last hour looking for Alice's Yorkie. She snuck out of the back door and made a beeline for the park and her favorite male beagle friend."

"You're such a good sheriff for the people in your town," I replied with a smile. The thought of Liam running around the park for a small dog who had no intention of being caught until he'd had his fun was rather endearing. "Did you end up saving the doggie from the dangers of an unsupervised park visit?"

"Brownie is safe at home and curled up in front of a fire on her bed that probably costs more than mine," Liam replied wryly. "That was nice of you to help out Beetle today. I know he was worried that some of his clients wouldn't understand if he had to ask for a few minor delays in submitting their taxes this year. He reassured them that all returns would be filed by the established deadline and that no one would have to pay a fine due to the date their return was filed."

We spent the next ten minutes talking about Heidi coming to town for the weekend and a few extra days next week to help Beetle reconstruct his files. I also touched on the fact that she was bringing some very talented IT technicians who might be able to recover everything Beetle had been working on prior to the fire. It wasn't until the palm of my right hand began to warm ever so slightly that I realized something was going sideways.

I wasn't the only one, either.

Unfortunately, I had no choice but to remain outwardly calm so that Liam didn't know there was potentially danger heading our way. This was one of those frequent times that I wished for the freedom to tell him the truth.

Leo woke up as if an earthquake had occurred, scrambling to find his footing.

Is it the coven? Have they finally come for us? Where's that flamethrower?

Leo shook his head and blinked several times before falling back on his haunches in confusion. He looked a little worse for wear as he attempted to take in his surroundings, and that was saying something.

"...glad to hear that things with Heidi are progressing. Jack will be relieved to know that she's moving out of the city and out here where they can spend more time together."

I was trying to find out what the cause of my unease was that would have both me and Leo sensing what I could only presume was a threat. Like my ability to cast spells, my awareness of danger wasn't always spot on.

Leo yawned as he tried to sweep the cobwebs away.

The bell above the door chimed once more, and Liam turned to see who had entered. Seeing that he was standing directly in front of me, I leaned to the side just a tad.

You're right. Your spidey senses were off once again.

They certainly were.

I'm going back to sleep. You can leave that flamethrower in the armory.

"Liam, it's good to see you." Rye Dolgiram had entered the shop and was rubbing his hands together to get rid of the cold. He wasn't a danger, per se, but there was something about him that set off Leo, my mother…and me. Leo had followed him around one morning, and nothing was found other than the man had a decent work ethic as the town's handyman. "Raven, I was hoping to speak with you in private if you have a moment."

To say that silence had descended over the tea shop was an understatement. I'm pretty sure that the ringing in my ears had nothing to do with the bell above the door.

I'm now fully awake for this visit. Wait. Do I have time to throw a bag of popcorn in the microwave?

"Of course," I replied hesitantly to Rye, completely ignoring Leo. This situation was uncomfortable enough without me having to hear Leo's snarky play-by-play. "Liam, if you'll give me just a—"

"It's okay." Liam might have said it was alright, but I could see his curiosity about why Rye would want to speak with me in private. Liam was opting to leave instead of requiring me to step to the front of the store to speak with Rye. "I have some paperwork to finish up at the station. I'll see you later."

Ouch.

Since when did chasing down a dog for a resident require paperwork? I decided that wasn't important, but there was something a bit off about letting him leave without…

I unconsciously wrapped my fingers around Liam's arm and stopped him from turning away. It was easy to lift up on my toes with the knee-high black boots I was wearing and press a soft kiss against his cheek.

Well, this is a bit awkward.

Sure enough, a quick glance toward Rye showed me that he was shifting his weight as he looked back out the glass door to give Liam and I some privacy.

"Thanks for the drink," I whispered, still wanting to keep our little secret about him sneaking me coffee between us. Maybe I *should* cancel the order I'd placed this morning. "Call me later?"

Hey, can I be on a team? You remember those Twilight books and how there was a Team Edward and a Team Jacob? I'm just not sure who I would go with…Team Liam? No, you shouldn't be with a human. It only causes trouble. Team Rye? Not a chance. He's too secretive. For all we know, he could be a werewolf.

Werewolf?

I distinctly remember Leo mentioning that there were no such things as vampires, werewolves, or things that go bump in the night. Well, with the exceptions of ghosts. Considering we had an up close and person visit from an apparition, it was safe to say there *were* things that went bump in the night.

You got me. I don't remember that conversation, but I can only assume that I said some of those things so as not to overwhelm you.

I made a mental note to stock up on garlic and silver. I'd have to have a small panic attack later seeing as I was currently about to have a conversation with a man who had been nothing but secretive since I'd met him.

After Liam promised to call me later, he walked past Rye with a respectful nod. The bell chimed once more, eventually fading while I stared at Rye and waited to hear what he could possibly want to speak with me about privately.

I could name a few things, but I have a somewhat twisted view on such motives.

I'd first met Rye when a storm had stranded Heidi and me in town one night a couple of months ago. A window had been broken by a branch that had fallen off a tree, and he'd come to temporarily fix it so that we could finish riding out the storm without losing too much heat at the inn.

Leo and I had both gotten the sense that there was something dangerous about the man, but we'd never been able to figure it out. As Leo had mentioned, the man was secretive. Mysterious would probably be a better adjective.

You left out tall, dark, and handsome. I believe those were Heidi's words, not mine. I personally don't agree with that assessment.

There was some truth to Heidi's adjectives, but it wasn't like I was attracted to Rye. I wasn't, and I had no plans to seek him out.

The lady doth protest too much...I think.

I wasn't protesting anything. Liam was the man who'd been in my thoughts every second of the day ever since I'd moved to Paramour Bay. Granted, we'd only been on a handful of dates, but the man had a way of making my heart flutter that no other man could do...including the one standing in front of me.

"I was hoping to talk to you about Gertie," Rye said, taking a step closer.

That's it? And here I thought this was going to be some explosive moment. I'm going back to sleep.

"I saw you stopping by the inn earlier. Did you notice anything amiss with her?"

"Gertie?" I asked, just to be sure we were talking about the same person.

The older woman had seemed in great spirits, although a bit lonely considering that the guest list this time of year was a little thin. My palm was still tingling slightly, but it wasn't burning to the point that my subconscious believed I was in danger.

"I'm worried about her," Rye disclosed, the small shrug telling me that he was a bit embarrassed about his concern. It hadn't been my intention to make him feel uncomfortable for being worried. "Gertie has been calling me over to the inn for issues that don't need to be fixed. I get the impression that she's lonely, but Beverly still goes over every day to help out with the meals and laundry."

"Gertie seemed fine, and she even invited me in for some tea." I recalled my short visit and nothing stood out. "I didn't notice anything wrong, but then again, I wasn't looking for a problem."

Rye nodded, but he didn't seem convinced. He even parted his lips as if to say something, but he seemed to think better of it. Now I had a sense of despair at not being able to help him. He wasn't even related to Gertie, yet he was checking on a fellow resident and making sure she was okay.

I couldn't let him leave without reassuring him that I would help out any way I could and even visit Gertie again.

"Rye, wait," I called out, taking the few steps between us when he'd turned to go. I'd noticed once before, but his eyes weren't technically brown…though they were dark in color. They were as dark of a green as they could possibly be without being black. "How about I check on her tomorrow? Maybe the holidays brought her down. I know that she doesn't have any family, and that can definitely be a damper at these times of the year."

Rye gave me that crooked smile I'd seen him give numerous other people, but he was always so serious around me. Maybe that's why I thought he had something to hide.

"Raven, I wasn't going to bring this up," Rye said hesitantly, his grin fading when he tried to come with a way to tell me something that I obviously wasn't going to like. "I probably shouldn't say anything at all."

"You can't leave me hanging now that you brought it up."

"Well, I know this is going to sound really far out there," Rye began, once again stopping short of telling me the true purpose for his visit. I had a horrible feeling that this was right on par with me possibly being responsible for the fires. "It was the reason I didn't want to discuss this in front of Liam, but I knew you'd understand."

"Understand what?" I asked cautiously, somehow ending up gripping my coffee cup to the point the lid was ready to pop off. "Rye, just spit it out."

"I stopped in unexpectedly at the inn last night to check up on Gertie and saw her…"

Dancing naked under the full moon? Willing down moonshine?

Leo was awake, in case you didn't notice.

Who could sleep through this part of the story? We're getting to the good stuff now. Do you think Rye caught Gertie with matches and a can of lighter fluid?

Gertie had to be in her nineties, so it was doubtful the woman had been running around Paramour Bay setting fires in the back alleys of the shops or to offices off the main thoroughfare.

Don't forget Beetle's house.

Something was bugging me about that misplaced blaze, but I couldn't focus on anything but what Rye was about to reveal.

"Rye? What did you see?"

I'm on pins and needles here, and it's not withdrawal from my supply of catnip.

"Raven, I swear I saw Gertie performing some type of…voodoo." Rye ran a hand over his face in astonishment, but he couldn't have been as stunned as I was in this moment. Gertie wasn't a witch. At least, I didn't think she was a witch. "It's a well-known fact that your grandmother dabbled in holistic medicine, but this was…this was different. It's why I'd thought I'd ask you for your opinion. Maybe she has lost her grip on reality."

Well, Heidi did find some pestles and mortars in the woman's kitchen the night of the snowstorm. Gertie even hinted that she knew of the Marigold secret, not that she has any concrete evidence. With that said, I'm here to tell you that our dear old inn keeper is not a witch.

"Voodoo?" It was the only word I could get out around the constriction of my throat. I had to cough to get out a full sentence. This was not where I'd thought the conversation was heading. "What, exactly, did you witness with your own eyes?"

Rye shook his head in denial, but he finally shared the details of his discovery.

"Gertie was lighting some type of green silver leaf on fire and tossing it into a bowl with other ingredients while candles were lit all around these weird metal bowls." Rye shoved his hands inside his coat pockets with a shrug. "I never went inside, so I couldn't hear what she was saying. I never let her know that I was there and a witness to whatever it was she was doing. I just left."

Fire? A green leaf from a silver maple? Where would that old innkeeper find something like that this time of year? I hate to say this, Raven, but I might have to retract my last statement.

I almost yelled out to Leo that he didn't need to say anything, but I caught myself just in time. Rye had thrown me for a loop, and I needed time to process all these new details.

What's there to process, Raven? It's simple—you might not be the only witch in town.

Chapter Eleven

HAVE I MENTIONED that this is an exceptionally bad idea? I just wanted to go on record.

"I'm taking the next logical step," I muttered behind the scarf that I'd wrapped around my face. Five o'clock had finally rolled around, giving me the chance to stop in at the inn. I'd have to come up with an excuse that I lost an earring or something, but at least it would get my foot in the door to do a little investigating of my own. "Gertie can't be a witch. You would have already known that little detail, along with Mom and Nan. Remember, Mom did live here for some twenty-three years before moving away to New York City."

Hello? Are you conveniently forgetting that I have a memory problem?

"I'm not forgetting anything," I argued, hurrying down the sidewalk now that it had started to flurry. "Please just stick to the plan I laid out. I'll try to find out all I can about the leaves and herbs that Rye saw Gertie lighting on fire while you search through the kitchen."

Was it possible that Gertie was a practicing witch? What could she possibly gain by setting fires around town? It made no sense, and I wanted to check this out myself so that I could rule out such a preposterous notion.

Is it preposterous? Gertie is somewhere in the range of mid-

nineties. Sure, she uses a cane...but she sure can get from one place to another with ease.

Leo did have a point. If Gertie had been Nan's customer for the same arthritis blend that she'd made for Otis, then why hadn't Gertie come to me for the same holistic remedy?

Witches don't need another witch to make their own magical blends, do they?

I completely understood where Leo was going with this conversation, but something just wasn't right with our train of thought. A simple visit to Gertie could alleviate any more suspicion. As it stood, Liam was searching for a culprit in these arsons. Unfortunately, he wouldn't find one if the fires were the result of witchcraft.

I had no choice but to investigate Rye's claims myself.

Speaking of Rye, did it ever occur to you that he completely made up a story about Gertie just so that he could talk you into this course of action?

"Here we go again," I grumbled, grateful that we'd finally arrived at the inn. Leo's theories about Rye were over the top. At least the walk had done me good and cleared my head of doubts. This was a simple check on a neighbor, and my visit would finally ascertain if Gertie had been keeping a secret from the town for over nine decades. "Leo, Rye has no interest in me nor I him."

You keep telling yourself that, princess.

I carefully made my way up the steps to the inn, mindful of any ice that might have escaped the sand or salt Gertie had put down after the last snowfall. I'd closed the tea shop at exactly five-o'clock, but the sun was still shining. Now that it was February, dusk had been pushed back just a little.

"Remember, search the kitchen," I reminded Leo, opening

the heavy wooden door. I was still uncomfortable with such an act, but this was a B&B—the entrance was always open. That sweet fragrance I loved so much hit me the moment I crossed the threshold. "Here we go. Wish us luck."

Closing the door behind me, I noticed a guest sitting on the ornate couch with a computer positioned in front of him on the coffee table. I'd heard that Mayor Sanders had a state official stopping in sometime this week, so he must have arrived early.

"Raven, is that you, dear?"

"Hi, Gertie," I called back after pulling my scarf down around my neck so that she could hear me. Sure enough, the older woman was making her way across the dark hardwood floor with her cane. "I'm glad I made it before dinner."

Along with the sweet fragrance that always seemed to linger in the air, the smell of various delicious spices could be detected from the kitchen. As I'd mentioned before, Paramour Bay wasn't quite the tourist town in the winter months. The guest in the formal living room was probably the only individual with a room, but with his reservations came free breakfast and dinner service.

"Beverly is putting the finishing touches on her famous fettucine alfredo as we speak." Gertie still continued to shuffle her way toward me as I hung up my dress coat and scarf. "Would you like to join me in the kitchen?"

"How about a cup of tea?" I compromised, knowing she meant dinner. Gertie never ate with her guests, preferring to take her meal in the kitchen. "I just wanted to check in with you."

"You can visit me any time, Raven," Gertie gushed in generosity, slowly turning to make her way back to the kitchen. I fell into step with her, sliding my purse back over my shoulder. I found it odd that Leo hadn't said anything since I'd come inside.

Was he experiencing a memory snafu? "I've reprinted off those financials records and made new copies of my receipts for Joseph. I was going to have Beverly drop them off at his house, so your timing is perfect."

I was still stuck on the name Joseph. It was easy to connect the dots, but I'd never heard anyone call Beetle by anything other than his nickname. He had filled out his tax forms as a subcontractor in order for me to be able to pay him and have the monies declared as income, but I never scrutinized them that closely.

Please don't judge.

I was still getting used to this small business owner thing. Plus, I hadn't cut Beetle his first paycheck.

"Do we have another guest, Gertie?" Beverly called out from her place by the oven. She was busy cutting a loaf of fresh baked Italian bread she had buttered and toasted with garlic salt and placing the piping hot slices inside the cloth napkin lined basket. "I've made more than enough if I need to lay out another place setting."

Beverly Garber worked part time at the inn cooking and housekeeping, but she was also friends with Cora. I was always careful about what I said around her, though she'd never given me any reason to believe I had to watch my words too closely. Truthfully, she was a really sweet woman.

"Raven stopped by to have a cup of tea with me," Gertie said enthusiastically, causing my guilt senses to trip. With that said, the palm of my hand remained cool. I honestly didn't believe for one moment that she was a witch. "I'll put on the kettle."

"How are you doing, Raven?" Beverly didn't once break stride with her preparations. "I heard about the fire in the alleyway behind your shop. Cora said there was no damage done to her place, but she said that you weren't so lucky. I hope you didn't lose too much inventory."

"Just a few items that I'd had opened in the back room, which thankfully wasn't a lot. To be honest, you could say that I'm being overly careful by discarding anything that wasn't sealed." I took a seat at the kitchen table, having already done this a time or two. Gertie loved getting her guests tea, and it was best to leave her to it. A quick scan around the elaborate kitchen didn't reveal anything unusual. "With all the smoke out back, we'd thought the fire had been in my storage room. Come to find out that it had been coming from a trash bin located too close to the building."

"I'm glad that no one was hurt."

"It's just horrible what's been happening around town." I internally cringed at the ease in which covered what might very well be my own misconduct. "First the tea shop, then Monty's hardware store. Beetle's house, his office, Oliver's office, and we can't forget the pub. I just don't see why those places were targeted."

"I'd heard the pub was a false alarm, but I understand what you mean." Beverly covered the bread with another cloth napkin to keep it warm before proceeding to check on the pasta. She not only had prepared fettucine alfredo, but she topped it off with a bubbling layer of melted cheese by baking it in the oven for just a bit. "I know the Owens, and Billy is a good kid. He might have been a handful when he was younger, but what child isn't? I feel bad for Bree Stonehedge, though. I heard someone at the diner this morning say that she might have needed the insurance money for the debt her ex-husband left her with on his way out of town."

Bree Stonehedge was the owner and operator of the small

bakery in town. I found it odd that she only had the shop opened in the morning hours, but I'd never had a full conversation with her to ask her the reasoning on that business decision. She didn't drink tea, and I seldom saw her around town after noontime.

Either way, Bree didn't strike me as the type of person who would break the law for financial advantage. We weren't discussing a speeding ticket here. Arson was serious business, and defrauding an insurance agency was also a major felony.

I also found it rather strange that anyone inside the diner would accuse Bree of such a horrible thing, but gossip did have a way of traveling through the gutter. Usually, the residents were really kind to one another and would never make unfounded accusations.

"Here we are," Gertie said, having set a tea pot on a tray with two cups and saucers. She had to have gotten the assembly from the tea shop, because I recalled a similar set in the inventory. "I'm so glad you stopped by, because I've been meaning to ask you something."

Where was Leo when I needed him?

We had come up with a plan, and he'd been going to search the other side of the kitchen I couldn't see from my position at the table. I'd give him a few more minutes before resorting to plan B…not that I knew what that was at the moment.

"You can ask me anything you need," I responded with a smile, glad to have some filler until a decision had to be made. I reached for the sugar, spooning out a healthy scoop before adding big pour of milk. "Have you run out of tea bags for your guests? We're getting a few new flavors of tea for the spring and some gourmet coffee grinds with an assortment of French presses."

Gertie went about fixing her tea as she obviously tried to figure out how to ask me what she wanted to know. I suddenly became rather uncomfortable, but not to the point where the palm of my hand became warm. She was taking too long to speak, and the drawn-out pause set me on edge considering the original motives for my visit.

My thoughts immediately went to something innately personal...like my relationship with Liam or the fact that I came from a long line of witches, but that was most likely my imagination running wild.

Right?

I froze when lifting the cup to my lips, because Gertie had leaned in close as if she were about to discuss a top secret. Oh, wow. She *was* going to ask about one of those two sensitive topics.

"Your grandmother taught me a few holistic remedies, Raven," Gertie whispered, letting her gaze land on Beverly who was still standing in front of the oven. "I know they were old family recipes handed down over the generations, but I haven't been sleeping well lately. I attempted to make a tea blend the other night, but it didn't turn out so well."

It was a good thing I hadn't taken a sip of my tea. What did Gertie mean by Nan sharing special Marigold remedies? Was this elderly inn keeper implying that she *was* a hedge witch? Had Nan helped her along her journey as Leo was doing for me?

Or was Gertie simply speaking the literal truth in regard to holistic tea blends?

"I won't be long," Beverly called out as she opened the oven and pulled out her fettucine alfredo. My stomach didn't even rumble at the delicious aroma that wafted over to the table. I was still struggling on how to answer Gertie. "I'm serving dinner to our guest, but I'll join you ladies for a cup of tea in a few minutes once he's served."

Gertie and I both waited for Beverly to exit through the other doorway that led to the dining room, not having to worry about her walking past the kitchen table. I can't even begin to tell you how relieved I was when Gertie cleared up my misunderstanding.

"Rosemary had given me a few tea blend recipes for relaxing the mind and body. I'd written down the remedies, but I spilled some water on the paper and smudged the last ingredient." Gertie reached over her tea cup and saucer for a loose piece of paper that had been tucked into a recipe book. "I know that you've taken over your grandmother's holistic medicine side business. Do you think you could help me figure out what I'm missing?"

"Of course," I replied with sheer happiness that I hadn't walked into something that could have been major trouble...especially seeing as Leo had abandoned me. Truthfully, I was becoming a bit worried. "Let me take a look."

I bit back a smile when I realized that Nan had told Gertie to mix a bit of nutmeg into her chamomile tea. Gertie hadn't been creating her own tea blends, but instead had been mixing two remedies together. Nan had even told her to light candles when mixing the two ingredients, creating what some would call a placebo effect.

Unfortunately, this remedy didn't explain why Gertie had been lighting something to drop into a pestle. Was she playing me? Was I falling for the innocent elderly lady routine? Was she aware that she had been observed while casting a spell?

"I also had to burn a silver maple leaf and some sage to ward off unfavorable spirits," Gertie whispered with a nod of satisfaction, taking me by surprise. "You grandmother was a very wise woman, Raven. I've lived in this house my entire life, and I've seen things no one would ever believe. It wasn't until Rosemary came along with that little sage burning trick that I was able to rest easy about roaming spirits. The silver maple is my family's signature leaf. We were originally French Canadian, and my family moved here during the 1790s after the war."

My relief was once again vast, and I was grateful I'd taken time out of my day to clear up some misconceptions. I'd be able to explain Gertie's odd behavior to Rye, all the while knowing that Gertie wasn't some evil hedge witch who was setting fires all around Paramour Bay.

"The ingredient you're missing for the holistic sleep remedy is fresh ground nutmeg," I shared, finally able to enjoy my tea. Don't get me wrong. I totally would rather have had coffee, but I was remembering to take the smaller pleasures in life—such as knowing there wasn't dark magic at work here in Paramour Bay. "Nan was a very wise woman, and I'm very glad that she shared with you that burning sage can cleanse a house of any unwanted malevolent spirits."

We continued to talk about other holistic remedies, though I was very careful to stick to the basics of what I'd learned over the last four months. Witchcraft did incorporate medicinal herbs, and that's how the holistic movement originally gained momentum. Some minor treatments were actually hedge witch recipes. Having such knowledge was a blessing.

Unfortunately, I was still in the dark as to whether or not I was responsible for the arson in this town that I'd come to love. There hadn't even been a report of a lighted match to indicate that I'd rectified my blunder. Granted, it was great that no other fires had been set, but the overwhelming guilt was enough to have me falling at the tips of Liam's boots to confess.

Good gracious, you don't have to go and be that melodramatic. Besides, I can confidently assure you that Paramour Bay has an arsonist in its midst...and you're not going to like hearing the name of the guilty party.

By the time Leo had arrived, Beverly was sitting across from me and enjoying a cup of tea while waiting for the guest in the dining room to finish his dinner. I'd gotten rather good at hiding my reaction to Leo's presence, so I didn't even startle upon hearing his response.

That didn't prevent me from tightening my grip on the tea cup in anticipation of Leo's announcement.

I just witnessed Chief Mason toss a lit cigarette into an outside garbage can with my very own eyes!

Chapter Twelve

"LEO, WE ALWAYS get into trouble when we start assuming things," I chastised, parking my beat-up old Corolla outside the wrought-iron fence that lined our front yard. "Chief Mason smokes, but he did not toss a lit butt into the trash. He made sure the cherry was out, and he didn't even litter. The man is an upstanding citizen of Paramour Bay, and you were ready to throw him under the bus on next to no evidence."

Before Leo and I continued with our conversation, let me quickly describe the exterior of my beloved cottage. It sat on a large piece of property overlooking the water on the far edge of town. My closest neighbor had to be a half mile away. The land between my place and the edge of town could best be described as thickly wooded wetlands.

No matter how eerie the outward curb appeal of my plot of land looked to the other residents, I thanked Nan every day for giving me this place and the life that had been hidden from me.

Sorry to interrupt, but the reader needs to be reminded that your mother is to blame for not disclosing the Marigold secret. Rosemary wanted you to know what you were missing from the time you were still in diapers. Carry on.

You see, the outside of the cottage resembled something out of a 1950s horror film. The overgrowth of tangled thorns—which had lost all of its leaves due to winter—had climbed up the front façade in an ominous manner. The wrought iron fence had spikes on each rail, while the two stark trees on either side of the pathway looked ready to reach out and grab the first unwanted person crazy enough to attempt entry.

You really need to cut down on those old black and white horror flicks. Those piercing screams put me on edge.

Thankfully, the interior was something entirely different. It was as if the place had popped right out of a home décor magazine. Nan had truly had a way with style, but I might have to spruce up the outer appearance with some landscaping and a fresh coat of paint on the house. I couldn't have Liam driving out here and believing that I didn't take care of my property.

The good ol' sheriff shouldn't be driving out this way at all. He should be keeping his distance. You're going to slip up one of these days and land us in hot water with that guy. That reminds me, the spell to reverse memory is on page three hundred and twenty-six...just in case you need to clean up one of your spells.

"It's been going fine so far," I reminded Leo, shutting off the engine before grabbing my purse. "Better than you wandering off and abandoning me at the inn. What if Gertie had been a wicked old hedge witch who dabbled in black magic? What then?"

I saw something down the alleyway that needed to be investigated. How was I to know the cigarette wasn't lit when Chief Mason tossed it into the trashcan? You said yourself that it was probably someone tossing matches or some such trash in the garbage cans. I can't help it if you plant your idle seeds of doubt into my head. You're like a disease.

I didn't bother locking my Corolla as I headed for the gate. It might be better all around if someone stole it.

Of course, that was highly unlikely. First off, no one ever

came out this way. Second, the crooks wouldn't even steal my hunk of junk back in New York City. I did have the feeling that the reason Nan had kept the outside of the cottage looking so menacing was to keep the locals at bay.

On second thought, I hope nobody stole the old girl. I couldn't bear to part with her just yet.

In my defense, I was in and out of the alleyway before you finished your cup of tea. And it's not my fault that you tripped over me when we went back to the scene of the crime. You made a scene with your clumsiness. If you'd pick up your feet just a bit, I bet that wouldn't happen on a reoccurring basis.

If you're thinking that I had subsequently snuck behind the alleyway of the volunteer fire department to check out their trashcans for myself, you would be right. Fortunately, my sleuthing skills were getting slightly better, and I was able to get away before anyone saw me snooping.

Regrettably, my accident-prone tendencies had gotten in the way of a quick getaway from the sidewalk out front where Richard had spotted me as he'd been walking toward the front entrance.

Poor man. He was mortified.

I winced at Leo's recall of the situation, though my reaction might have been more about the biting wind coming off the waterfront. It truly was cold out tonight.

Anyway, while the sweet fireman had been helping me to my feet, he attempted to apologize for his odd behavior the other day. He went on and on about how he wasn't sure what had come over him.

I, in turn, had feigned ignorance on the entire subject. Richard's relief had been evident, but my guilt had only ratcheted higher. It seemed everything going wrong lately had been connected to my spell failure.

Don't fool the reader, Raven. You got over your remorse of flubbing that spell quickly when Richard fessed up that the fire department had put out another blaze this afternoon.

It was true.

My self-doubts had been mostly erased the moment Richard had admitted to taking another 911 dispatched call to a fire behind the bakery. There had been no need for the lights and sirens, because two of the volunteer firemen had been inside the bakery when the patrons smelled smoke. Don't think I didn't recall what Beverly had said about Bree Stonehedge.

I also found it odd that the bakery had been open after twelve o'clock in the afternoon.

Since when had Bree decided to have evening hours?

Could the bakery owner be the guilty party?

Had Bree Stonehedge just been using other small fires to throw off the trail of local authorities?

If it looks like a duck…

"Remember what I said about making assumptions?"

No need to be crass.

The lights were shining from the two windows, which told me that Ted was inside getting a fire started in the hearth. It was nice to come home and find that he'd warmed the place up. Coming home in the evening wasn't so lonely, and the cozy warmth immediately hit me after opening the front door.

"Hi, Ted," I called out as I set my keys in the wooden bowl on the entry table to my right. "How was your day?"

"It was good, Miss Raven."

Great conversationalist you've got there.

Leo had already jumped up on his pillow in the front window, causing him to be out of the way of my purse…which I'd swung in his direction to knock some sense into him.

"Thank you for getting the fire going this evening." It didn't take me long to set down my purse, hang up my dress coat, and switch from my knee-high boots into my fuzzy slippers. "We have a lot of work ahead of us this evening."

You didn't clue the reader in on your epiphany.

"It was a good epiphany."

Using a destroyed item in a spell isn't what I would call a good epiphany.

"Leo seems upset," Ted pointed out, taking the herbs and roots out of the basket he'd set on the coffee table, separating the ingredients into tiny bundles.

All Ted could hear was Leo meowing, just as any other human would. Ted wasn't exactly human, as we all know. Ted's lack of understanding made it hard to carry on a three-way conversation, but we were getting used to it.

"I'm casting a spell on the ashes that were left behind from the fire in the alleyway behind the tea shop." I walked across the hardwood floor to the kitchen which was also done in modern décor. I especially appreciated the new stainless-steel appliances. As I'd mentioned, Nan's home interior design was impeccable. "It appears I'm not responsible for the fires around town. Or so it would seem."

"I never thought you were, Miss Raven."

Suck up. I swear, he's such a lapdog.

"It seems that there are rumors around town that Bree Stonehedge might be responsible," I shared with Ted, completely ignoring Leo. He was currently cleaning his paws, still trying to get rid of the lipstick mark left by the fairy we'd saved on our last case. "I can't imagine such a sweet woman doing such a thing, and a divination to find the guilty party might be able to clear her name."

Have you ever thought that it could be someone from the coven? Maybe someone stirring the pot here in Paramour Bay?

I'd gone about getting a bottle of wine out of the refrigerator and had been in the process of pulling the cork when Leo made such an outrageous suggestion. Yes, we'd had run-ins with the council. Yes, there had been talk of an upcoming war between factions of the coven my family had once been members of...but we'd been excommunicated many years before I was ever born. There was no reason for them to involve me in their internal issues, just as there was no reason for them to bring their battle here to Paramour Bay.

"Who are your suspects?" Ted asked, finally finishing the task of sorting the ingredients he'd brought in the basket.

Look at good ol' Crayola getting in on the sleuthing action. What color would you say he is? I'd guess dull grey, maybe.

"How's that spot on your paw coming along, Leo?" I asked, showing him that it wasn't nice to make fun of others.

My comment was said in affection. You're just being spiteful.

"No, it wasn't," I countered with an arched eyebrow that didn't even come close to rivaling my mother's. I'd managed to pull the cork and pour myself a glass of wine. It was time to settle in and find a spell that could help put away an arsonist before Valentine's Day. "Ted, that's a good question. We thought it was Billy, especially considering he was at two of the fire scenes. Then Gertie entered the picture, but we quickly put an end to that theory...thank goodness. Now, there are rumors that Bree Stonehedge might be responsible, because she needs the insurance money."

"Miss Bree wouldn't do something so terrible."

That's what neighbors say about every serial killer in existence—

she was always so quiet. Right up until she burns your house to the ground with you in it.

"I agree, Ted." I snatched up the grimoire and sat down on the couch, completely ignoring Leo. I was also careful not to spill my wine. It was time to dig into the volume of spells and find one that could guarantee my date tomorrow night would be a success. "Are you staying for a while? It's nice to have the pleasant company."

"I have dinner plans."

Well, Ted's announcement certainly had the crickets chirping around the room.

Don't ask.

I wouldn't ask.

Mindy's boutique was closed, which meant Ted wasn't having dinner with the mannequin he fancied in town. It was best to leave well enough alone.

"Have a good night, Ted," I called out tentatively, taking a healthy sip of my wine after he'd shut the door behind him. "Leo, I hope we don't end up with another emergency on our hands."

He's a walking, talking crayon. What harm could he get into?

I stifled a groan at Leo's ability to dare Karma to do her best and took another sip of my delicious wine.

"Ted has a point about a list of suspects," I pointed out, opening the leather-bound grimoire. I began to leaf through the pages one by one, hoping a divination spell would catch my eye where I'd be able to use the ash I'd collected from the garbage can out back of the tea shop. There had to be some spell that would point us in the right direction of a suspect. "Billy and Gertie have been discounted, so that still leaves Pete, maybe Sam, and Bree…although her involvement is based on nothing but rumors. You know that I don't put any stock into that type of human-spun gossip."

Did you ever think there's some truth behind those rumors? You—not me—are assuming that someone is lighting fires to get a thrill of watching things burn. What if there's a deeper motive behind the crimes?

Leo might very well be onto something there. Why were the fires being set if the blazes turned out to have nothing to do with my blunder? Did someone have a personal vendetta against the shop owners of Paramour Bay?

More importantly, who would benefit?

You know what, Raven? I think that premium organic catnip that Beetle has been giving me is making me smarter. I might very well be turning into a next level genius! You know, like that movie with John Travolta…only without the brain tumor!

Chapter Thirteen

"YOU'VE STIRRED UP quite a ruckus, my dear Raven," Beetle exclaimed as he breezed through the front entrance of the tea shop. "Quite a ruckus!"

It was a good thing I'd loaded up my travel mug with coffee, because Beetle's enthusiasm was more than my caffeine deprived brain cells could take this morning. I'd stayed up late looking through the family grimoire for any type of spell that could use ash left behind by the guilty party…and came up with less than zero.

Don't get me wrong.

I'm sure there's a divination in those pages somewhere, but there were literally thousands of spells to comb through. I wouldn't give up my search, but it was postponed until tomorrow when I could pick up where I'd left off.

Today was Valentine's Day.

And tonight was reserved for me and Liam.

At least, I still believed my special dinner with Liam was still on the schedule for tonight.

That reminds me that I'll need to find another place to smoke my pipe later this evening. Your plans are interfering with my personal reflection time, Raven. We really need to do something about this newfound relationship with the good ol' sheriff.

"I thought you weren't coming into work for a while, Beetle." I'd clearly heard that fact somewhere in the last few days. "And I'm not sure how I could cause a ruckus when I just flipped over the open sign."

My evening is ruined due to your need to rut around with Liam, and now you're trying to throw a wrench into my breakfast? Stop chasing the poor man off.

Catnip wasn't breakfast, but I was pretty sure that Leo would disagree with me on the subtleties of my point right now.

"Bree Stonehedge is quite upset that you're going to be selling gourmet coffee blends here at the tea shop. Quite upset," Beetle shared, busy trying to pull something from the pocket of his winter coat. "I'll have you know that we've gotten quite close over the past two days, ever since she allowed me to occupy a couple of her tables as a workspace to discuss my client's returns with them. My office still hasn't been cleared of the debris, and I simply cannot work from home. No, siree, Bob!"

If he keeps rambling on like this, I'm going to need double my usual fix this morning. Could you please relay that message to him, Raven?

I wasn't going to do any such thing, but I was quite concerned that Bree was upset about my new idea to incorporate coffee into my shop's inventory. This small bit of insider information was going to take some time to ponder, so I took a seat on the stool behind the cash register to think it over.

"I guess I hadn't thought of what my new business concept would do to the other shops in town who carried the same fare." I frowned when I mentally put myself in her shoes. "The diner is where most people grab their coffee while having breakfast, and the bakery is where the residents sit down to enjoy a quick cup of joe with a pastry."

"Precisely," Beetle stated, holding up a finger while the other hand victoriously held up a sealed bag of Leo's catnip. "I advised Bree to come talk to you sometime today to assure her that your intent was not to cut into her pre-established revenue stream."

It hadn't been my intention to cut into anyone's anything, but businesses expanded and evolved all the time. I'd already placed the order for my new inventory items, and they were scheduled to be delivered early next week. It was common knowledge that a business owner had to be cutthroat from time to time, but that just wasn't in my nature.

Besides, it wasn't as if the gourmet coffee niche was her bailiwick. She served a classic Columbian roasted coffee with her baked goods. My selections covered that type of roast, but I hadn't restricted myself to that blend alone. When all was said and done, we'd offer over twenty blends, and they would span a much larger spectrum of mild to rich flavors.

I had planned to offer one or two sample blends prepared fresh every morning, but I had intended to rotate through the entirety of my available selections to improve sales of the different blends. People looking for baked goods would still drink her coffee on the go, and they would stock up their favorite home grounds from what I offered here at the shop.

Would you stop distracting the man? I can smell that delicious, mouthwatering plant from here. Have we discussed a raise yet? Those extra dollars would certainly go a long way toward reimbursing this fine man for some of his premium stock.

"What I currently have planned won't hurt Bree's profit line at the bakery." After thinking my business plan through a little more, I was confident that I could continue as planned. "I'm not a café…yet. My expansion into coffee is with gourmet blends and the devices and machines that can create the perfect cup. Yes, I'll have two samples blends available for my customers to try, but they'd have to go to either the diner or the bakery to buy a regular cup of coffee."

That's right, Mister Supplier. Come closer. Just a little bit closer.

"My, oh my," Beetle crooned as he opened the bag of catnip and began to dispense the green leafy substance onto Leo's bed in the display window. "Aren't you affectionate this morning, my good ol' buddy?"

I am your buddy, Beetle. Your very best buddy ever.

I could literally hear Leo purr from all the way to where I was sitting behind the cash register. The only other person who had ever been able to make him purr was Heidi, but that was because Leo fancied himself to be love with my best friend.

While Beetle fawned all over Leo, I gave more thought to how Bree heard I was expanding the tea shop into more of a specialty tea and coffee shop. I shouldn't be surprised that my conversation with Trixie yesterday had already made the rounds. Bob Abbott was known for his love of Bree's chocolate frosted Bavarian cream filled donuts, and Alice probably hadn't wasted any time filling her husband in on the fact that I was going to include coffee beans and various grounds to my inventory.

"Bree was told that you're closing the tea shop in its entirety and opening a café like the ones seen in movies with the quaint outdoor cloth-covered tables from the French stylings of the 1920s," Beetle said after leaving Leo in peace to enjoy his morning treat. My part-time employee was repeatedly snapping his fingers to try and jog his memory. "What was that comedy show from back in the day? The one with all the friends?"

"*Friends*," I replied, technically not surprised that the rumor had been twisted around until the truth had all but been buried alive.

"Yes, the one about friends."

"*Friends*," I replied once more, putting a little more emphasis on the title.

Beetle cocked his head to the side, his white hair somehow remaining straight upward.

Be nice to the man, Raven. I'm not sure I could live without his daily visits.

"The television show was called *Friends*," I reiterated with a bit more information. Beetle's blue eyes finally lit up with understanding. "And I wouldn't want to own a café, per se, due to all the complexities it entails. But to-go cups of a rotating selection of coffee flavors wouldn't interfere with any other business in town. Besides, I can supply her with any grounds she prefers at a reasonable price."

Maybe we should consider adding a few feline pet selections...

"Good to know, my dear Raven. Good to know." Beetle stretched out his arm, inadvertently pulling back his coat sleeve so that he could see his watch. There was a huge clock behind me hanging on the wall, but he never looked at it. It made me think that no one else could see it, either. I made a mental note to check the timepiece for magical components. "Now, I must go back to work. You really need to try Bree's coffee cake. Delicious, just simply delicious!"

Beetle left just as quickly as he came, my hand still up in the air to wave goodbye as the door swung closed behind him.

The poor man is reduced to working across a few tables in a bakery. You really should have offered to clear the back storage area for him. He could have monitored my supply of catnip more closely from there, you know.

I pondered over Beetle's predicament, wondering what else he'd heard while working at the bakery. That place had to have been just as good as the diner for the day's fodder. Could he have possibly overheard something that would point Liam in the direction of his elusive culprit?

Isn't it odd that there was a fire here during Beetle's part-time hours, at his home, at his office, and now at the bakery...where he has temporarily set up an office? Poor man. The devastation seems to be following him around town.

Leo continued to consume the small mound of catnip that Beetle had poured out onto his bed while I sat back on the stool in disbelief. I'd been so caught up in believing that I may have been responsible for the fires, that I had completely missed Beetle's connection to the crimes.

I was still staring at Leo with incredulity when he sat back on his haunches and ogled down at the catnip as if it had come from the supply of "holistic" remedies I had in the storage room for some of the townsfolk who still hadn't stopped in for their orders. His left eye practically bulged out in astonishment.

This stuff does, in fact, make me a genius!

"I wouldn't get so carried away there, Einstein," I countered back, though I did give him credit for coming up with a theory of how the fires were linked. "How do you explain the small blaze behind Monty's hardware store? Beetle was still here when that occurred."

Hold on. Let me munch on this grand treat some more. I'm sure the answer will come to me. Talk about a secret weapon. I wonder what the afterlife is saying about my powers of observation now.

"Then there was that false alarm over at the pub," I shared, wondering if that particular 911 call had any substance. "Maybe it's a stretch to assume it's all about Beetle."

Have you ever heard of a criminal throwing off the authorities by diverting their attention? It happens on occasion, you know.

"Are you saying that Beetle himself is the one responsible for setting the fires?" Leo stopped eating long enough to look my way, our gazes meeting in heavy doubt. "You realize that I'm going to have to mention this to Liam, right?"

No, no, no, no, no. We will do no such thing, Raven. Remember, Beetle supplies the inspiration for my genius intellect. We're just going to have to figure out a way to throw the good ol' sheriff off of Beetle's trail. It's what any good friend and employer would do, right?

Chapter Fourteen

CAN'T WE HAVE just one chapter start where I'm not telling you that your plan is a bad idea?

"We have already had some of those," I argued, having waited all morning to close the tea shop for lunch and walk over to the bakery. Beetle had said that he'd suggested Bree come talk to me, but why wait when I could give her some peace of mind…especially if she was worried about the bakery's revenue. "Besides, I'm not doing anything that could stir up any more trouble. I'm simply walking over to the bakery—devoid of any malice, I might add—to speak with Bree and maybe join Beetle for some of that coffee cake."

I thought we were in agreement that Beetle wasn't responsible for the fires, but that the fires might be related to Beetle in some way.

We'd spent the morning debating on whether Beetle could actually be responsible for the arson problem, but it just wasn't that likely when we knew who we were dealing with. Beetle hadn't left the tea shop the entire time he'd been working that particular day. Trust me, I'd given him numerous times to bail on the part-time gig, but he hadn't gone for it. Moreover, even if we believed he was the culprit, it would have been impossible for him to be in two places at once.

Unless Beetle had access to the same astroplane evocation you used to bust in on that council meeting of the coven.

"Stop being ridiculous," I mumbled, believing it might be best to leave Leo behind at the shop. I grabbed my purse from beneath the counter, noticing the glaringly obvious hole in the cubby where I'd been keeping the heart-shaped glass container. Dee hadn't had time to stop into the tea shop yesterday, but she'd quickly breezed in and out this morning. "Why don't you go take a walk around town and see if you notice anything out of the ordinary."

You'd like that, wouldn't you? Well, neither one of us is going anywhere. It seems my catnip might have taken on some unique properties...such as the ability for conjuration and summoning.

Sure enough, a quick look out the display window showed me that Beetle was headed this way. I was concerned with the way Leo announced his presence.

"Leo, you do know that your catnip is just a dried weed and not a spell component, right?"

That's what you'd like me to think, isn't it? Good luck trying to pull one over on me.

"My dear Raven," Beetle called out as he walked through the door with one hand in the air. "I didn't want you to worry about our conversation this morning. I had a heart to heart talk with Bree, and she's ecstatic that you're not going to open up a café. Even better, Bree might decide to expand into that arena and was hoping that you'd be the one to sell her the gourmet coffee you'll be carrying here in the shop and the various items she'd needed to get started. Seeing as I do the taxes for the bakery, I'm very familiar with the finances of such an adventure. I've run the numbers, of course, and you'd both make a nice profit. A very nice profit, indeed! Why, Leo would have a lifetime supply of catnip if this pans out."

I didn't think I could love this man any more than I already do.

The church should offer him up for sainthood.

"Take your time looking over these," Beetle suggested, handing me a manila folder. He turned right on his heel and made a beeline for the door. "I'm off to see Cora about those receipts I never received. No time to waste!"

Catastrophe! I don't get my noontime snack? Raven, call him back this instant!

"Beetle, wait," I called out, hoping to slow him down. As an employee, I didn't fault him for wanting to expand my business, but this was a big step. I needed time to look over the numbers, just as he'd suggested, but there was also the issue of his involvement in the fires. "I wanted to run something by you."

And me! Ask him if he has any more catnip in his pockets.

Beetle clicked his tongue against the roof of his mouth as he glanced toward the ceiling, clearly calculating how much time he could give me. I made sure he'd want to stay and hear me out by stating the truth.

"Beetle, I think you might be the cause of the fires."

Be still my racing heart. Did you just accuse the man of arson? Have you lost your ever-loving mind?

"You believe that I—" Beetle covered his mouth in horror. Both of them had taken my statement out of context. "I'm horrified, Raven. Just horrified."

I just thought of something more horrifying. What if someone actually wants Beetle dead?

"Beetle, of course I don't believe you started the fires," I clarified, setting down the manila folder on the counter before making my way around the cash register. "I'm saying that the fires are connected to you. Think about it. You lost your office, you almost lost your home, and then there's what happened in the alleyway."

Gasp! They were attempts on his life by some antiliberty movement bent on destroying the free use and distribution of catnip! Raven, I'm in total agreement now. We must stop this travesty of justice!

Beetle's white bushy eyebrow rose, causing some of the loose strands of hair on his head to do the same. It was clear he hadn't previously entertained the idea that he might be related to the offences occurring around town, not that I blamed him.

If this were a television show, they would suspect the spouse. As much as I love the man, no one in their right mind would marry him. He does have more than a few screws loose. That leaves his work. He must have unearthed proof someone is embezzling, and they want him dead!

Leo was certainly on a roll. There was going to come a horrendous time when I would have to limit his catnip intake, but as for right now…he really was coming up with some fantastic motives for arson.

I credit the catnip. Beetle must buy his stuff on the black market.

"Beetle, is it possible that someone wanted to burn down your office and home to get rid of some kind of evidence…maybe of some sort of financial corruption?"

"I did bring my briefcase with me to the tea shop that morning," Beetle shared, frowning as he thought over the last few days. He tapped his chin. "And I did set it inside the back room."

"Did you recently find something wrong in anyone's accounting? Maybe something off with their books?"

That's a HIPAA violation, Raven. He can't reveal that type of information without a warrant. Are you trying to get this man in more trouble?

I had to bite my tongue to correct Leo's mistake. HIPAA was

for the medical field, not for financial records. That didn't mean there wasn't some law against Beetle disclosing someone else's business records. I suppose it most likely had to do with business/client confidentiality.

"I'm saying to think it over," I advised Beetle, wanting this done the right way. Liam would probably want his Ts crossed and his Is dotted for an arrest. "If you remember anything at all that would indicate embezzlement or something even more serious, you need to go to Liam. I know that he's been working around the clock to find the guilty party."

Does that mean the good ol' sheriff might not be coming to dinner?

"I know all of my clients personally, my dear Raven." Beetle shook his head in remorse before laying his hand over his heart. "It would pain me to believe that someone I've known for years would resort to such drastic measures to destroy evidence of a crime. Why hand over their financial records at all? They also could just as easily have altered the books before giving them to me."

He has a point. Maybe we should invite him inside the van for a chat.

I'd become accustomed to Leo's quips, but that particular one had me so confused that I couldn't prevent my gaze from swinging his way. He was certainly a sight, with his crooked whiskers this way and that. There must have been a little catnip left over, because there were a few green flakes stuck to his bottom lip.

The Scooby Doo van, Daphne. Not the mobile library van.

Wow. Sometimes Leo's brain went a bit faster than I could handle.

Keeping up with Leo on some of his more obscure references

was like following Dennis Miller on one of his Monday Night Football rants. The juice just wasn't worth the squeeze at some point.

"Leo, my good feline, aren't you looking spry this afternoon? I'd heard that catnip can help with weight control." Beetle winked my way as if I were in on his little secret. "We'll have you looking fit as a fiddle in no time at all."

The only part of Leo that moved was the end of his tail...you know, the three-inch section that was bent like a hanger. I'd come to know that type of twitch, and he was debating on whether or not to attack or defer.

Give me a minute to decide.

"Leo does love the catnip you sneak him every morning," I said, purposefully reminding Leo that Beetle was technically his weed supplier, for what it was worth. "I read somewhere that catnip is good for their memory, as well."

I've heard of this kind of love/hate relationship, but I've never experienced it before. I don't think that it is a healthy arrangement.

Beetle certainly did have a way with backhanded compliments. We were getting way off topic, though.

"You have a point on the financial records, Beetle." It didn't make sense to hand over evidence of a crime, only to then try to destroy it. "Have you upset anyone recently?"

Why, yes. Yes, he has. I can come up with one most recently.

Leo would eventually get over the slight insult, most likely tomorrow morning when Beetle came into the tea shop with a new bag of catnip.

"My dear Raven, I go to great lengths to treat my clients with the utmost respect." Beetle hadn't removed his hand from his chest, but he did pat his fingers against his tie and rock back on his somewhat well-worn dress shoes as he contemplated my inquiry. "Always respect. Although, there has been a time or two when I've had to give advice my clients didn't want to hear. Not to the point where they would burn down a town, mind you. No, no, my dear Raven. I do not believe any of my clients would resort to arson."

Oh, well. You tried. Let's park the Mystery Machine and let the good ol' sheriff handle this one.

"I'm off to talk to Cora. I still need those receipts for the fourth quarter." Beetle waved his hand in the air as he spun around and headed for the exit. "Ta-ta!"

Chapter Fifteen

"LEO, COULD THE council be behind the fires?" I asked, restocking the infuser section of the tea shop. I'd been pondering on my latest theory ever since Beetle had left to go in search of Cora. "I'm not sure what their point might be, other than to cause chaos for a witch who wants nothing to do with the coven."

Technically, the coven kicked the Marigolds to the curb a very long time ago. You know, before there was a curb.

I checked to make sure I'd grabbed the right infuser before setting the box facing outward so the customer could see the merchandise displayed correctly. Wilma and Elsie had made a special trip into town after Wilma had accidentally thrown away her infuser. The two had stayed for quite a while chatting about the events around town, even chalking up Wilma's odd behavior to an allergic reaction to the new hair dye Candy had used at the salon.

You're going to put that poor woman out of business now that she has to order an entirely new brand of hair dyes. Way to support the local economy there, Raven.

"It's not like I can fess up to the truth before the entire town," I replied wryly, for a brief moment thinking that this was a way for the coven to force my hand in returning to Windsor. Could Aunt Rowena be the mastermind behind such a plan?

She'd mentioned needing the rest of the Marigolds when it came time for the war between the factions to ensue. "What if Aunt Rowena is the one responsible for stoking the local fires?"

Your great-aunt isn't a witch who plays around the burning bush, so to speak. If she wanted to gain your attention, she would have burned down the entire town with you in it.

Leo did have a point. If Aunt Rowena really needed my help, or even my mother's assistance, she would have arrived on our doorstep with her broomstick in hand and asked for it. Failing that, she would have ensured we weren't batting for the other side.

"It's so frustrating that I couldn't find a spell to help with this case," I muttered, straightening the box on the shelf. "If the council or any member of the coven isn't behind this, I still think it's related to Beetle somehow."

Leo suddenly gasped, alerting me to the fact that an idea had hit him out of the blue.

What if it's because of my catnip? What if it's magical weed?

"What are you talking about?" I asked in complete confusion, knowing full well I didn't want to know how his brain worked. "Leo, the fires around town have nothing to do with your catnip."

I told you the stuff is so good that Beetle must have gotten it off the black market. It could be enchanted! What if it's a type of new cartel that needs to burn the evidence of such a find? I mean, they could mass market that stuff and turn their operation into a legal entity that would control the entire cat population!

So much for the catnip making him smarter.

Movement across the street caught my attention, and I smiled when I saw Liam heading toward the intersection with two cups of coffee in hand. Even after four months, the man could still make my heart flutter.

Perfect timing. You hold the good ol' sheriff off while I check into this lead. We can't have the cartel getting rid of Beetle, even if the man does annoy me with those backhanded compliments of his. Hold down the fort, Raven!

Leo disappeared before Liam made it across the road. Even then, Leo would have had some additional time to skedaddle without being noticed. Somewhere between the intersection and the tea shop, Liam must have stopped to talk to someone. I didn't want to be rude and poke my head out the door to see who that someone was might be, so I finished replacing my inventory before walking back over to the cash register to file my receipts.

As for Leo, he was clearly wasting his time. There was no cartel who dealt in catnip, but I did have to wonder if Beetle hadn't gotten caught up in something more dangerous than keeping the books for the local businesses. I'd brought up a client fudging numbers, but what if Beetle was in on it and blackmailing one of the shop owners?

I was beginning to sound as loony tunes as Leo, wasn't I?

Liam finally passed by the display window, his dark gaze meeting mine through the glass. He lifted one side of his lips, but the lopsided grin didn't quite meet his eyes.

"I tried to make it over this morning," Liam said after entering the shop, careful not to drop either cup. "The day just got away from me."

"Did something interesting happen?"

I hadn't heard any sirens to indicate that there was a fire. That didn't mean there hadn't been another incident. Whenever Liam continued to walk my way upon entering the store, it meant he was here to stay awhile. He did so now, so I pulled the stool a little closer to the counter and settled in for what had become our daily chats.

"Happy Valentine's Day, Raven," Liam said softly, handing me one of the coffee cups. He'd somehow made the rest of the world fade away when he produced a single rose from the inside of his brown suede jacket. "I hope the events around town aren't going to interfere with our dinner."

"Happy Valentine's Day, Liam." I could so get used to this warm intimacy I experienced whenever he dropped his voice an octave…which I would have said was impossible. I brought the rose up to my nose and inhaled its sweet fragrance. The touching offer made me want to close the shop now and head for home. "And dinner is still at seven o'clock as originally planned."

Liam held up his coffee cup until I clicked my lid with his, both of us taking our first sips of the rich beverage with huge satisfaction.

"Wilma and Elsie stopped in a bit ago, and they didn't mention anything," I shared once we set our cups down on the counter. I continued to hold onto the rose, loving this small gift that told me Liam had thought about me this morning. "After you share the details of your day, I'll share mine."

I couldn't perform any spell that would give us the answers to the questions we all had, but I could run my ideas past Liam in hopes that I could help with the investigation. Our long-awaited Valentine's Day was finally here, and I wanted tonight to be perfect.

"There is a pattern to the fires, and I wanted to talk to the shop owners before drawing any conclusions." Liam leaned an elbow against the counter as he settled in. I loved this time with him where we just talked about our days and learned more about each other. "As a matter of fact, I just ran into Cora. We're meeting in around thirty minutes after she has a small powwow with her managers. Roger will have to call in, though. He's still cooped up with the flu. A lot of the shop owners are having to reprint their financials after they were destroyed by the fire at Beetle's office."

"That's what I wanted to talk to you about." Had Liam come to the same conclusion as I had in regard to Beetle's involvement? I twirled the stem of the rose in my fingers before checking to see if there were any thorns. Thankfully, Liam must have had the florist remove them. "What pattern did you discover?"

Liam regarded me carefully, the way he did every now and then that had me wondering if he saw more than I wanted him to in regard to my family's secret. A smile slowly formed on his lips that had me breathing a bit easier.

"Are you applying for the position of deputy? I might have to run that one by Oliver."

"I'd make you a great deputy," I replied with feigned indignation, causing him to laugh out loud. "Wasn't it me who helped Detective Swanson solve the murder over at the inn?"

"You mean when the murderer came to your room to try to kill you?" Liam's brown eyes somehow became even darker at the memory. He shook his head when I started to argue. "I swear Jack almost gave me a heart attack when he called to tell me what had happened in your room. I'm warning you now...any application for a deputy position that comes across my desk with your name on it is being fed into the shredder immediately. You had me worried sick with your antics."

It was so sweet to know that Liam had a protective streak a mile long. Regrettably, he had no idea the power I held in the palm of my hand. According to Leo, Liam could never know of my abilities as a witch. I'd broken one of the major rules of the coven once before, and I could do so again—against Leo's wishes, of course. I just wasn't so sure Liam would ever view me the same if I did.

Let's face it, witchcraft was scary business and not to be bandied about lightly.

"Liam, I took self-defense classes in the city. I'm perfectly capable of taking care of myself if need be," I assured him, deciding now was the time to bring up my theory. "Take for instance this pattern you think you've discovered…it involves Beetle, doesn't it?"

I could tell from his expression that I was right. Liam had made the same connection, but I still couldn't understand why Monty's hardware store had been targeted by the perpetrator unless it was to throw off anyone who made the same connection.

"Liam, did you know that Beetle had brought his briefcase with him to the tea shop the same morning the fire broke out in the alleyway? I think whoever set the fire thought the flames would either make their way into the storage room or that we'd be forced to vacate, thus giving him or her the freedom to retrieve the briefcase."

"I spoke to Beetle at length the day multiple fires broke out around town. I began to put the pieces together after his office was targeted, but it became rather clear when the bakery was hit soon after that." Liam sighed and pinched the bridge of his nose, as if he shouldn't be sharing this information with me. It was technically an ongoing investigation, but it was nice to know that he trusted me with these small details. I didn't have to tell him I wouldn't say a word to anyone, because he already knew that in his heart. "Everyone had to vacate the building, including Beetle. Bree had given him a couple of tables in the back of the bakery where he could work in private with a client and not be disturbed, but Chief Mason cleared out every patron from the building first thing when he arrived."

"Leaving Beetle's files on the table open for anyone to see who might sneak back inside the bakery without anyone noticing," I said, filling in the rest of Liam's theory. A spark of excitement shot through me that we were on the same page. This was similar to when Leo and I worked together, only this was bit more exciting in terms of this newfound relationship. "I was thinking that maybe a client was doing something fishy with their financial records, but Beetle pointed out they wouldn't have given him the real books to begin with if they were embezzling or trying to avoid paying their fair share of taxes."

"I was thinking along those same lines," Liam said before taking another drink of his coffee. He rested his elbows on the counter as he leaned down to share his thoughts. "What if the evidence of such a crime was given to Beetle by mistake? What if they handed in the wrong set of books? My only concern is that I personally know every shop owner in Paramour Bay. These are serious allegations, and I need to tread carefully. We're talking multiple felonies here."

"Who do you think it could be?" I asked, having tried to narrow down the suspects. I couldn't come up with anyone who could be such a horrible person. Well, Cora wasn't all that nice of a person, but I would never label her as someone who would resort to actual criminal behavior. "I was talking to…Ted about this last night. We tried to come up with suspects, but you're right about us knowing everyone personally. We couldn't pinpoint anyone, either."

I almost messed up and mentioned Leo. Liam would have definitely thought I was some type of lonely cat woman, not that I would have had a problem with that. Leo beat out a lot of those people in New York City who I would never have called a friend.

I needed to fib a bit on this next part, but Ted and Leo were almost interchangeable in my life as it was. I loved them both.

"Ted said something that stuck with me, though." I fiddled with the rose so that Liam wouldn't notice my apprehension in misrepresenting the one who mentioned this small detail. "No one ever thinks their neighbor could commit such horrible acts, such as serial killers. The newspapers almost always mention the same old quote about it being the quiet ones."

"True," Liam acknowledged with a tilt of his head. "That's why I have to remain impartial. I also can't assume that it has to be a client who is the guilty party. A lot of these shop owners don't handle the day to day operations of their shops. Many of them have managers."

The bell above the door chimed to signal I had a customer, but a quick look revealed it was Cora.

Speaking of the devil herself.

Cora was technically one of those shop owners Liam had just mentioned, and she had one of her managers do the nightly bank deposits, among other such duties. Could it really be that simple?

Could Roger Aimes be the guilty party?

I don't think so, Raven.

I continued to smile at Liam as he gathered his coffee and bid me goodbye before pausing next to Cora at the door. The way she shot me a sideways glance told me what she thought of Liam and I spending time together during the workday, but her opinion didn't matter to anyone I knew. A quick wave and the two were eventually on their way.

It wasn't long until Leo physically appeared on his pillow in the display window.

"Leo, what do you mean you don't think Roger is the guilty party? Who else do you think it could be?"

I think Beverly was right about Bree Stonehedge. I was checking on Beetle at the bakery to make sure that the cartel hadn't gotten to him, and I might have accidentally walked into the private office in the back.

"Might have? Accidentally?" I hopped off the stool, knowing full well I wouldn't be able to share this information with Liam without having a valid reason why I was in possession of such evidence…whatever that evidence may be. "Leo, weren't you the one who lectured me on the random violation of people's privacy?"

I also pointed out that there were exceptions…such as Beetle being abducted and tortured by the catnip cartel. I bet they're a vicious group known for their hideous torture techniques.

"Leo, there is no catnip cartel," I said in exasperation, wondering just how far he was going to go with this dramatic tale. "Beetle buys your catnip from a pet store in New Haven."

Leo blinked a few times as he absorbed the truth I'd just blurted out. Trust me, there were times I believed that the coffee I was drinking also had powerful magical properties.

You do realize that is something you could have told me before I believed I was risking my life for a man who thinks I'm overweight and have the appearance of Frankenstein's feral cat.

I shrugged, ready to admit that I never knew how Leo's mind worked.

We can come back to that later. Right now, we need to convince the good ol' sheriff that Bree Stonehedge is the one lighting those fires around town.

"Leo, what did you find in Bree's office?"

A safe full of cash…stacks of cash. I'm not talking about a few extra five dollar bills, either. There had to be at least several hundred thousand dollars inside with multiple passports. I cracked the case, Raven. I'm a freaking genius!

Chapter Sixteen

IT'S TIME TO bring in the good ol' sheriff and let him do his own job for once.

"And how am I supposed to steer Liam toward Bree as the arsonist?"

Was Leo right in his assumption that Bree had been embezzling money from her own storefront? She could have a ton of reasons for keeping that much cash on hand in her safe. The passports gave me pause, but I'm sure someone would find the way I ran things here at the shop a bit odd, too. There were still things that didn't add up, though, and I did agree with Leo that the situation warranted more investigating.

A safe full of cash and multiple passports. What more evidence do you need?

"Maybe Bree is saving the money for a reason, and you said yourself that you didn't see whose pictures were inside the passports," I pointed out, pulling out the white garbage bag from the small trashcan next to the sampling table. "It could be her family's passports. Maybe she keeps everyone's documents locked up for safekeeping."

It was four-forty, and I was very tempted to close up early. I still had to prepare a Valentine's Day dinner for Liam and make myself presentable, as well as hide all the tangible evidence that I practiced witchcraft at home. Oh, and I needed to make sure the grimoire was tucked away in its own special drawer inside the coffee table. One that couldn't be opened by anyone who wasn't of the family bloodline.

Just so you know, both of Bree's parents are dead.

"Oh, that's so sad," I exclaimed, sympathy building up for the bakery shop's owner. My mother might drive me crazy at times, but I couldn't imagine not having her here with me. "That makes what we're accusing her of even worse. What's to say that Bree just couldn't bring herself to destroy their passports? Leo, we've learned time and time again that things aren't always what they seem."

I'm pretty sure we assumed correctly that you were to blame when half the town was seeing floating hearts.

I remained silent as I drew the navy blue strings closed so that the garbage bag was easier to carry toward the back room. There was no obvious approach for me to give Liam the lead to catching the Paramour Bay arsonist without revealing my little witchcraft secret. It was best I leave well enough alone tonight and come up with a plan tomorrow to find a spell to prove Bree's involvement. Now that we had a suspect, maybe I could use some type of divination spell to prove her guilt.

Well, when you put it like that...the reader will think we're awful people.

"You're a cat, Leo," I muttered, parting the ivory-colored fairy beads so that I could reach the seldom used back door. Flipping the deadbolt, the cold hit me with a force. I was only taking the trash out to the bigger bin, so I didn't bother with a jacket. "Oh! Hi, Sam."

Sam?

Oh, yes. Sam, the young and innocent-looking teenager, stood next to the malt shop's trashcan. It had been clear that he'd been rummaging through the contents. He'd shot straight up so fast that he almost slipped on a slick spot.

Hmphf. Reminds me of you.

Leo hadn't bothered to conceal his presence. He was sitting on his haunches taking in the exchange before him just inside the doorway where I'd left the heavy door open.

"Ms. Marigold!" Sam attempted to smile, when it was more than clear he'd been caught in the act of...well, I wasn't sure what he'd been doing in the garbage. "Here. Let me get that for you."

My fingers immediately released the white trash bag when he took it from my hand, more because I had become rather cautious of his motives.

Didn't you say he had an innocent smile?

I did, and I also trusted my instincts. The palm of my hand remained cool as Sam lifted the lid to the metal garbage can alongside the brick wall.

"A wise woman knows when to change her mind," I muttered, pasting a smile on my face when Sam turned back after throwing the small trash bag into my garbage can. "You look concerned, Sam. Is everything okay?"

Sam shifted back and forth on his running shoes, as if he were debating whether or not to bare his soul. It was more than evident that something was bothering him. Unfortunately, Bonnie appeared in the back doorway of the malt shop.

It's like a convention of misfits.

"Sam, the computer is still down," Bonnie complained, giving me a quick wave and dismissive glance. "You're going to have to tell Cora that we won't be able to print those receipts today. I'll go ahead and make the nightly deposit at the bank before they close while you lock up the shop."

Oh, Beetle won't be too happy to hear that. This delay is going to cost me my daily catnip, isn't it? Those computers are going to be the death of me.

"I thought Roger dropped off the bank deposits?" I'm not sure why I blurted out that question, but it had fallen off my lips before I'd even realized I'd spoken. My attempt to appear disconcerted by my nosiness fell flat. "Sorry. I didn't mean to overstep. It's just that I heard Beetle mention it the other day."

You're getting as bad as Elsie and Wilma.

"Well, Roger has been out with the flu," Bonnie said with a bit of irritation, not that I blamed her. It wasn't any of my business who made the nightly deposits for the malt shop. "This is the third day he's called off."

Interesting. I guess it wasn't Roger who wanted to visit Cancun, after all. Who knew that Bonnie was the type of person to hang out with scaly lizards?

Sam gave me a small shrug before turning on his running shoes and once again stepping on the slick spot that had almost landed him on the ground the first time around. He went down like a ton of bricks.

Mother Nature 1…Sam 0.

I was the first to reach Sam, leaning down to make sure he hadn't hit his head on the cement. He was wincing and groaning in pain.

"Are you okay?" I asked, wondering why Bonnie hadn't joined me in trying to help Sam to his feet. Honestly, it was usually me who ended up on the ground and needed a little TLC. I wouldn't ever wish harm on anyone, but it was kind of nice not being the one to draw attention. "Here. Let me help you up."

"I think I broke my ankle," Sam complained with a grimace,

sitting up enough to grab his foot.

Raven, it looks as if you're going to have to cancel your dinner plans and take Sam to the hospital. I wish I could take the credit, but good for Sam for stopping a mistake in the making. Just how were you going to explain that coffee table and all the hidden locked drawers? Your date is in law enforcement. It's in the man's nature to be curious. Oh, well. It's better this way.

"The bank closes in ten minutes," Bonnie complained in an unusual manner. She'd always struck me as sympathetic, but at the moment…impatience ruled. She shifted on her feet, and her agitation had nothing to do with the cold. "Sam, try to stand. I'm sure it's just a sprain."

She's one of those "rub some dirt on it" kind of gals.

It didn't escape my notice that the palm of my hand had begun to tingle. Something wasn't right with this situation, but I couldn't quite put my finger on the problem.

I'm pretty sure it's because you just set your hand down on some ice for a bit of balance.

"I'm sure Cora will understand why the nightly deposit didn't get made under the circumstances, Bonnie," I exclaimed, ignoring Leo as I tried to make sure I didn't also go down in a heap next to Sam. Couldn't Bonnie see that it was going to take the both of us to shift Sam off the ice and to his feet? "Do you think you could help?"

I didn't mean to come across as rude, but was it too much to ask for a bit of compassion? Bonnie audibly sighed her resentment for being made to stay later than she'd apparently wanted to on this Valentine's Day.

Did you ever think that Bonnie has a date with Billy? You might not be the only one with a hot date lined up for Hallmark's favorite holiday, Cupid.

"What on earth is going on here?"

I should have commenced a drumroll upon your nemesis' entrance into this vaudevillian scene. In my defense, I didn't know Cora would be the spoiler in this chapter.

By this time, both Bonnie and I were struggling to get Sam to his feet. It wasn't easy, and Sam's inability to bear weight made the progress even more difficult. Cora was already halfway to us when by happenstance a brochure with a rather large green iguana fell out of Sam's apron and spiraled in the cold air until it gently landed at the tips of Cora's dress boots.

All of us stood there quietly staring down at the…

Evidence. It's okay to accept that the one most unlikely person in this scenario is the guilty party. Happens all the time in those best-selling mystery books.

Sam?

He was only nineteen years old.

How could someone so young have pulled off stealing from a business while at the same time hiding plans to leave town?

I'll say it—he was always such a quiet boy. Do you think I'll get interviewed for the Paramour Bay Gazette? Even better, the mayor may finally give me a key to the town.

"It's not what it looks like," Sam exclaimed in innocence as Cora leaned down to pick up the travel brochure. Bonnie stepped to the side, leaving me the only leverage for which Sam had left to stand. "I didn't steal anything from you, Mrs. Barnes!"

That's what they all say.

I have to admit that I was taken aback by how easily Sam would deny being guilty of a crime, all because of an innocent little brochure. No one had accused anyone of anything at this point, yet he was claiming innocence before there had been any finger pointing.

"Steal? It was you all along? How could you do this to me, Sam?" Cora asked in disappointment, clearly making the same connections that I had with regard to the fires. "All for a Caribbean vacation? Stealing money from the shop is one thing, but those fires could have really hurt someone."

Oh, well. It looks like the good ol' sheriff is going to be busy with a lot of paperwork tonight. What shall we have for dinner, Raven? I was thinking of marinated salmon grilled to perfection with a sauce made of pasted anchovies.

"I didn't set any fires, Mrs. Barnes," Sam denied emphatically, hopping slightly when I shifted my weight to pull my cell phone out of my skirt pocket.

Leo had a point about calling Liam, though that didn't mean our dinner plans would be ruined…just pushed back a little. I still found it rather odd that I hadn't sensed any threat coming from Sam when I'd first come out to the alleyway.

"Sam, how could you?" Bonnie shook her head in disappointment when Sam began to protest even more. "I thought something odd was going on with you lately, but this?"

I had programmed Liam's cell phone into mine, designating him a favorite. It didn't take me long to find the right screen, so all I had to do was press the button.

There's a twist coming, isn't there?

"Raven?" a sweet voice called out, causing all of our gazes to swing to where Leo was still sitting just inside the threshold. His tail twitched and he bared the longer fang as a pretty woman with long chestnut colored hair appeared behind him. "I'm Bree Stonehedge. I was hoping to speak with you about your expansion into coffee. Um, is everything okay out here?"

Dun dun dun! I've always wanted to do that!

I wasn't exactly sure what Leo was leading up to with his imitation of the scary movie reveal, but I was certain that we all appeared rather odd to Bree with everyone glaring at Sam with disappointment and me struggling to keep him upright.

"Aunt Bree?" Sam called out, practically sagging even farther into me with relief, but all I could do was a double take.

Aunt Bree?

Ahhhh, I knew there was something I forgot to tell you. They're related.

Chapter Seventeen

"WHAT EXACTLY IS going on here?" Bree asked in confusion, taking in the small gathering of people before her. She frowned with concern. "Sam, did you hurt yourself?"

Don't trust this woman, Raven. She has a safe full of cash, multiple passports, and a nephew who could easily have been the arsonist to help save his aunt from a lifetime spent behind bars. Orange appears to be her color, after all. Liam could probably book them under the RICO Act. It's a huge criminal conspiracy, you know.

A quick look informed me that Bree was wearing what I'd call a burnt orange colored scarf with her black wool dress coat. There was something off with this entire scenario, though. I needed to encourage everyone to move inside and call Liam immediately.

"They think I started the fires, but I didn't," Sam protested, hopping on one foot toward his aunt and not giving me a choice but to go with him. "I think it's Bonnie or maybe even Roger."

And the twists keep coming. Poor Roger is down with the flu, and he's being thrown under the bus as a sacrificial lamb. Hmmm. Lamb. That might be nice, with some mint sauce.

Don't worry, dear reader. I would never allow Leo to hurt a cute little lamb.

"What?" Cora and Bonnie both exclaimed in unison, although for very different reasons. I couldn't imagine trusting someone enough to help run the tea shop, going so far as to give them a management title, only to have them steal from the profits. "Bonnie, is this true?"

Shouldn't the good ol' sheriff be dealing with this kind of situation? I need to find us a lamb to roast.

"No, it's not true," Bonnie cried out, her eyes instantly filling with tears. She rested a hand on her chest in dismay, clearly stressed by such an accusation. "How could you think I would do something like that, Sam? Is that why you were acting so odd all day?"

Those tears do look real, and Sam does appear a bit guilty. But we can't forget about Bree...and her safe full of cash. Do you realize how much catnip I could buy with that pile of money? Think of all the benefits—you could fire Beetle, I could still maintain my genius-level IQ, and you can drink as much coffee as you want. I'm telling you that this a win-win situation all around.

I had a feeling that this was no-win situation. Someone was going to lose, because it was only a matter of time before the truth came out. As it stood, we were all way too close in proximity for my comfort level, so there was only one thing to do. I pressed the button on my display next to Liam's name.

Oh, good. You can tell him that dinner plans are cancelled.

Liam answered on the first ring, but there was no way that I was going to cancel our evening. I still had hope that this could all be resolved quickly.

Just remember page number three hundred and twenty-six in the grimoire. Trust me, you'll need it.

"We have a bit of a problem over here, Liam," I informed him after he'd sweetly asked if I'd run out of coffee. "It's about the fires and possibly theft. Could you come over to the tea shop? We'll all be waiting."

Why can't you all go over to the malt shop? I'm all sleuthed out, and I don't want to people anymore.

It had been best to clue Liam in that I wasn't alone here at the shop. Leo didn't want to hear this, but there was quite a bit more sleuthing to be done. We technically hadn't solved the mystery of who had been setting the fires, especially with all this finger pointing.

Honestly, I don't know which direction to look at the moment.

"Cora, do you think you could handle this?" Bonnie asked as she glanced down at her watch that had more colors in it than my peacock skirt. "I might be able to talk Nora at the bank into taking the nightly deposit seeing as it's only a couple of minutes past five."

I could totally visualize her as the Bonnie in a Bonnie and Clyde scenario. No one in their right mind would cast Sam as Clyde, though. Hmmmm. We do have more sleuthing to do. I can't have the afterlife believing I neglected my duties.

"No one is going anywhere until you all speak with Liam," I said assertively, indicating with a nod that Cora and Bonnie should go ahead of me and Sam. Truthfully, I didn't want to let anyone out of my sight, but Sam's inability to walk on his own had me slowing down just a bit. "Cora, you should call Desmond."

Good thinking. Good ol' Desmond could have been having an affair with Bree Stonehedge, devised a plan where his entire staff embezzled money from the malt shop, and intended to have all of them fly to Cancun so he could kill his co-conspirators while sailing away with Bree on a yacht.

I recently recalled Ted saying something about being hooked on afternoon soap operas. Leo must have popped in on Ted a time or two, because his version of what could have happened was a wee bit dramatic.

"Desmond is still out of town," Cora stated with a haughty tone. I hadn't meant anything by my suggestion, other than that he was part owner of the shop. Cora seemed to think I proposed she call her husband because she couldn't handle this situation by herself. "I'll speak to Liam myself and see that this is all straightened out."

"I'm sure you'll get your chance," I muttered, grateful when Leo had taken the lead and not-so-gracefully guided everyone through the storage room, through the ivory-colored beads, and into the main area of the tea shop. Sam and I were bringing up the back, giving me time to throw a few questions his way. "Sam, why do you think Bonnie or Roger are the ones who set the fire? If they talked you into helping them, just come clean with Liam. I'm sure he'll understand, and you telling the truth will only help your case."

I think what you're doing is called entrapment.

"I didn't have anything to do with the fires, but Billy and I were inside the malt shop when the first blaze happened," Sam confessed underneath his breath so that the women in front of us couldn't hear what he was saying. "Roger had come into the malt shop that morning, but he'd left within the hour because he hadn't been feeling good. That was the reason Bonnie had to work that morning."

You know, I never did like the game of Clue.

"Would someone please tell me what is going on?" Bree asked in disbelief, having waited right inside the ivory-colored fairy beads to help me navigate her nephew to a stool at one of the high-topped tables. "Sam, I'll call your mom. It's going to take her a while to get here from New Haven, but you really should have some type of proper representation."

You should tell Bree that she should take her own advice.

I wasn't going to do any such thing, and I was saved from having to get into a mental debate with Leo when the bell above the front door of the tea shop signaled Liam's entrance. I breathed a sigh of relief that he would now be able to sort through all the stories…one was guaranteed to be false.

Or most of them. I still think my theory about Desmond could be a real possibility.

"Would someone like to tell me what is going on?" Liam asked with a frown, his brown suede jacket framing his wide shoulders perfectly. His air of authority came naturally and was something to see, but our date hadn't officially started yet. It was best to help him crack this case so that our Valentine's dinner could still take place. "Raven?"

Do tell, Raven. Explain how you got us into this mess.

I couldn't help but shoot Leo an exasperated look before explaining what had taken place in the alleyway. It wasn't like I had purposefully exposed myself to an arsonist. Sam was all of nineteen years old, and it had been natural for me to commence small talk. I hadn't forced him to act odd enough for me to take notice.

You could have walked away, Raven. You could have walked away.

"I had been taking out the garbage for the evening when I saw Sam in the alleyway." I shrugged with a bit of an apology Sam's way, who was currently lifting up his injured foot on the other stool that Bree had moved closer. "I'm sorry, Sam. You were acting a bit strange."

Everyone in this town is at least fifteen percent strange.

"Because I think Bonnie or Roger has been stealing money

from the malt shop," Sam exclaimed, true panic written on his features now that he was being confronted by a police officer. "I swear, Mr. Drake. I didn't set those fires, but I've heard the stories about Beetle being the target. I put two and two together, and I'm pretty sure that Bonnie or Roger are—"

Leo and I were now swiveling our heads back and forth between those talking, every now and then focusing on Liam's reaction. With every second that ticked by, I could see our special dinner being postponed.

"Sam, how can you think that I had anything to do with something so horrible?" Bonnie cried out, casting a pleading look Cora's way. "Mrs. Barnes, I've been working for you since I was eighteen years old. I wouldn't steal from you. You're just trying to throw suspicion off yourself, Sam!"

Leo had made himself comfortable on the counter near the cash register. I had too much adrenaline flowing through my body to sit on the stool, so I leaned against the side and attempted to figure out who was lying.

It's impossible to say who is lying in this situation. It comes so naturally to them, doesn't it? You know, that says something about this younger generation—all out for themselves.

"Sam wouldn't make up a story like that," Bree countered, doing the honorable thing and defending her nephew. I did give her props for being loyal to her family. "Cora, you've known our family your entire life. You know that Sam would never steal from you."

That's what they all say.

"Everyone just stop for a moment," Liam ordered, remaining where he was, most likely in order to keep an eye on everyone. "I'll ask the questions. Cora, have you noticed anything amiss with the malt shop's receipts?"

Point for the good ol' sheriff for gaining control of the situation. I don't believe I give him enough credit when it comes to the detective side of his job.

Cora's hesitancy was enough to tell everyone that there might have been a problem.

"Beetle mentioned yesterday that he'd been thinking about the fires, and how most of them seemed to be when he was around," Cora explained warily, her sideways glance landing on me. I straightened my shoulders defensively, ready to protect myself. "It appears that Raven suggested the fires had something to do with someone stealing. Beetle told me that he'd only been able to glance at my paperwork, but that he noticed the nightly deposits being a bit short every now and then. He made a note to look deeper into the problem, but..."

Now the truth of it all comes out.

"Beetle never got around to it," Liam stated, clearly having already known this piece of information. "I'm not asking what your tax preparer's view is on your finances, Cora. I'm asking you if you're missing any money."

The good ol' sheriff doesn't mess around, does he?

Chapter Eighteen

I HAD TO admit, it was interesting to watch Liam in action. He still maintained his authoritative position by the door, although his tone reassured everyone in the shop that he would treat them fairly if they were honest with him.

The good ol' sheriff carries a badge, a pistol, and a pair of shiny handcuffs. If I were these folks, I'd be negotiating a deal right about now.

"Cora?" Liam prompted the woman, tilting his head slightly so that he could get a better look at her. She pressed her lips together in a combination of frustration and embarrassment. She clasped her hands in front of her, clutching the brochure she must have picked up outside before we'd ventured into the tea shop. "Do you have any reason to believe that one of your managers stole from the malt shop?"

"Desmond has been traveling a lot lately, and I've had my hands full with the ladies' auxiliary and the rental properties we own on the bay." Cora lifted her right hand to brush her rather stiff bangs to the side as she continued to give an explanation of why she hadn't been monitoring the malt shop's financials with a magnifying glass. An idea began to form which might very well allow me to have that dinner with Liam, after all. "There's a reason I hire competent managers, so no—I don't believe that either Roger or Bonnie stole from me."

Idea? No, no, no. The good ol' sheriff has this covered. We've completed our sleuthing abilities for the approval of the afterlife. There's no need to go past the point of no return...meaning our own deaths. One of these people might have a flamethrower hidden in their underwear. Oh, and did you notice the way Cora just threw Sam underneath the same bus that he was driving earlier? One should never leave the driver's seat unsecured.

"Thank you, Mrs. Barnes," Bonnie muttered, giving Sam a sideways look that clearly spoke of her forthcoming retribution.

If I were Sam, I certainly wouldn't drink any malts that woman made me anytime soon.

"Who does the brochure belong to?" I asked, causing all heads to swivel in my direction. Had no one considered the evidence? I realize that Liam hadn't seen the so-called proof that Sam thought he had found, but what if the young man had been trying to throw all of them off his trail? "Sam, is it yours?"

Bree Stonehedge looks more likely to me that she'd rather hang out with those scaly lizards than Sam.

"No!" Sam denied emphatically, grabbing ahold of his aunt's hand. Had Bree set her nephew up to steal the money with the promise of some extravagant trip? "I saw a few of them in the office over the past month, and then I finally put two and two together. I swear it's not mine!"

"It's not mine, either," Bonnie interjected, defensively wrapping her arms around her waist. "If you found it in the office, it could be Roger's brochure."

"Sam, please explain to me in detail why you believe that Roger or Bonnie would steal money and then try to cover up their crimes by trying to destroy the evidence," Liam coaxed, crossing his arms across his chest as he settled in to hear Sam's theory. "These are serious accusations you're making."

I couldn't believe I hadn't thought of this earlier, but if that brochure had anything to do with the reason why the money had been taken and the fires set to cover up the crime, there was a simple spell that would reveal who owned the brochure.

Spell? Simple? I was quite enjoying myself, Raven. Now you have to go and ruin a good whodunit show. You're liable to have every one of them on a plane in under an hour, headed for Lizard Island. I don't want to end up as collateral damage.

I quietly stepped back and made sure that I was behind the counter. The last thing I needed was for someone to hear me muttering a chant.

Chant? Oh, no! You aren't doing that aura thing again, are you?

I wasn't going to pry into the auras in this room, especially with Liam in the mix. I would have experienced guilt for my entire life had I betrayed his trust in that manner. No, I was going to cast a simpler spell that only required three lines. After Mom had explained the utility of using cantrips to my advantage, I'd done quite a bit of reading that night. I was more than pleased with a few of the cantrips I'd found, and one of them could be used right this minute.

No, no, it can't be used right this minute. I don't want to end up on Lizard Island! Those things eat cats there, you know!

You and Leo can rest assured that I wasn't going to make anyone go where they didn't want to go. The cantrip only included three lines. Even if said incorrectly, I'm almost positive that there wouldn't be any repercussions.

Almost? This is not a game of horseshoes, you know.

I flexed my hand to ensure that I could easily gather enough energy, mindful that Sam was still explaining why he believed one of the managers could be the arsonist. He still claimed that he wasn't the guilty party, thereby unknowingly declaring innocence on Bree. It wasn't like I could tell Liam that she had a safe full of cash and extra passports without revealing how I'd come by that bit of information.

Outing ourselves is sounding better than being eaten on Lizard Island.

All eyes were currently trained on the young man, freeing me to be able to cast the cantrip without anyone being the wiser.

You don't have to do this, Raven.

It was too late.

I was already drawing heat into my hand, allowing the energy from the earth to use me as a conduit. When I had enough potency to use the energy pooling within me, I began to mutter softly underneath my breath.

To whom it belongs
Let it be shown
Don't let the name be wrong

I never once let my focus stray from the brochure in Cora's grasp. If all worked out right, the name of the one who owned the brochure should appear somewhere on the glossy paper.

Over and over, I recited the couplet until Leo gave me the heads up that Sam was about done giving his account of Roger and Bonnie's concern over the malt shop's business during the winter months.

Well, we're all still here and in one piece. I don't have the urge to join the lizards, so maybe you succeeded in that bit of magic without sending these few occupants of this town into chaos.

"...not enough to accuse someone of stealing or setting fires around town, Sam."

"May I suggest something?"

I was a little bit out of breath, but sometimes casting spells did that to me. I didn't want to get off topic, but I was thinking about doing yoga again. Heidi and I used to take classes when I lived in the city, but no one had that type of business here in Paramour Bay. I should bring that up in our next town hall meeting.

Could we finish this story before you grow the town's chamber of commerce and advocate for more businesspeople? You realize expansion of the local community attracts more crime, right?

"Raven, this doesn't concern you," Cora pointed out, completely ignoring the fact that we were standing in my tea shop or the fact that my shop was the first to be damaged by the subsequent fires. She seemed to forget that I was the one who'd lost some inventory, and that my only employee was now working out of a bakery because his office had burned to the ground. "Liam, I've known you since you were a toddler. Would you please allow me to reach out to my husband and discuss with him what has taken place? I'm not even sure how this situation got so blown out of proportion."

Me, either. I think my short-term memory issue just kicked in.

"Sam was acting strange, and it was then that I saw the brochure fall out of his apron," I said, filling in the holes of the story so that Liam could follow along with what had happened here. "In Sam's defense, he immediately claimed innocence of any theft."

They all do…

"Cora, may I see the brochure?" Liam asked, holding out his hand and giving Cora little choice but to hand over the pamphlet. At least I didn't have to push the issue, because then I might have to explain how I was aware someone's name had been written on the paper. "Cancun? Do you know if any of your employees were…"

Ahhhh, he knows who wanted to go to Lizard Island.

I'd been holding my breath when Liam's voice finally trailed off. He'd conclusively seen the name of the person interested in going on vacation, but that didn't prove that he or she stole the money for the trip.

It does show that the employee has bad taste in vacation spots. Cancun isn't even an island, and it's pretty far from the Caribbean. These people really need to learn their geography.

I still had yet to inhale some oxygen, so my sharp inhalation could be heard the moment Liam announced the name.

"Bonnie?" Liam lifted his disappointed dark gaze from the brochure in his hand to the young woman. "Is there something you would like to tell me?"

Chapter Nineteen

"NO," BONNIE SAID, drawing out the last letter of her denial. I would have felt bad for her had she not gone so far as to set fires around town. Cora was right when she confronted Sam earlier about their potentially being someone seriously hurt by such a horrible deed. "I don't know what you're talking about. You know, the more I think about it…I'm pretty sure that Roger was talking about vacations. He could easily have set those fires. He's been out sick most of the week."

It's sad to see Bonnie try and wiggle her way out of this. Well, not that pathetic. She did almost burn up my stash of catnip. It's a good thing that Beetle keeps my supply at his house. With that said, she did try to burn that to the ground, too. On second thought, I'm not sad at all.

The other individuals inside the shop had no idea why Liam had suddenly focused on Bonnie, but it was now very clear to everyone present who was trying to lie her way out of the situation.

You realize this doesn't clear up the loose threads regarding Bree Stonehedge and her safe.

"Bonnie, you wrote your name on the brochure," Liam pointed out, holding up the evidence for all to see. He shook his head in disappointment, clearly having known her family for some time. That was the thing about a small town…everyone knew each other. "I'm going to ask that you come over to the station with me. Cora, you too, since it seems you've suffered some monetary loss. We'll contact Beetle and see if he can't pinpoint the errors on the receipts where I expect we'll find the lost revenue over the past month or two."

Look at that. Another mystery solved. Hey, go ask Bree why she has all that cash.

I wasn't going to pry into the woman's personal business. Bree Stonehedge seemed nice enough, and I could truly respect her inherent need to protect her nephew. So what if she kept cash in her safe and a couple of passports that might not even be hers?

If you must know, I do want an answer. I don't like unfinished business, Raven. You know this.

Another thing that reassured me that I wasn't a bad person was that everyone seemed to have their own little secrets. It made this whole witch thing a little more bearable.

"Liam, is it alright if I take Sam to the hospital to get his ankle looked at?" Bree asked, now that her nephew's name had all but been cleared.

"Of course." Liam tapped the brochure against the palm of his hand. "Just keep your phone handy in case I have any follow-up questions. And Sam? The next time you are suspicious of someone committing a crime, please come to me."

You might want to tell the good ol' sheriff that Bree could very well use those passports to avoid any type of future interview or interrogation.

I gave Leo a sideways glance, because we'd already decided that we weren't going to bring Bree's safe up to Liam.

You decided that all on your own…not me.

"I'm going home," Bonnie declared, a flush of anger steadily rising in her cheeks. "I did not steal any money, and I did not set any fires. And my name is not on that brochure. You're trying to trick me into a confession, and it's not going to work."

Poor Bonnie. She has no idea that she's already busted.

Liam arched an eyebrow as he held up the brochure with Bonnie's name clearly written in red ink. Somehow or other, magic had etched the letters into the paper for all to see. The supernatural never failed to amaze me with its mysterious ways.

"That's not possible," Bonnie whispered in shock. She even took a step backward, but there was no denying that the brochure was hers. It was like watching the hands on a clock tick by as the realization she was busted clicked in her mind. "Mrs. Barnes, I can explain. I was only borrowing the money. I was going to return every cent, I swear."

Wow, she's backpedaling like an Olympic cyclist, isn't she?

"Bonnie, why wouldn't you have come to me if you were in trouble?" Cora asked, her eyebrows into a V deeper than any valley I'd ever seen.

"Cora, I don't believe that Bonnie took the money because she was in trouble financially," Liam expressed his thoughts, holding up the brochure. "Bonnie, were you ever planning on coming back to Paramour Bay?"

The good ol' sheriff has her number, doesn't he?

"Why would I come back to a podunk town like this?" It appeared that Bonnie had finally given up the pretense that she wasn't behind the stolen money and fires. "If I'm going to work in a malt shop, I'd rather work at an ice cream shop in Cancun. At least they have beaches and sunshine to make it all worthwhile."

She'd do well on Lizard Island. After she gets out of prison, I mean.

I didn't understand why there were people in this world who didn't love the benefits of a small town, where there were townsfolk who relied on each other and looked out for one another. I'd been raised in New York City, and Bonnie needed to know that the grass wasn't always greener on the other side. Sometimes it was just more of the same.

I don't think Bonnie is going to need to know that particular detail where she's going. How many years do you think she'll get for all those felony arson cases?

"And the fires?" Liam asked gently, clearly knowing in his line of work that the longer he kept Bonnie talking…well, the more she'd confess.

"I was just trying to buy myself some time before Beetle found out the truth about the money," Bonnie admitted, tears filling her eyes. The waterworks weren't due to guilt, but more for the fact that she'd been caught. "No one got hurt. I even tried to throw Chief Mason off my trail by lighting the garbage on fire behind Monty's hardware store, but then Beetle had to go and ask everyone to reprint their receipts before I could get out of town. I was leaving for Cancun tonight."

Bonnie slid an accusing stare Sam's way, but his relief was evident that he'd proven his own innocence.

Is he innocent, though? Is he?

Leo was still trying to figure out why Bree had a safe full of cash, but that wasn't any of our business. The woman hadn't done anything wrong to warrant being revealed by our magically enhanced amateur sleuthing. Paramour Bay was safe once again, and I took pride that Leo and I had been a part of the solution.

I guess I never thought of it that way. I'm Batman, though. You can be Robin. Yellow is more your color than mine.

"The only place you're going is jail, Bonnie," Liam countered, motioning with his hand that Bonnie needed to go with him. He was nice enough not to use cuffs, but I had no doubt that the next few hours would be filled with paperwork, calls to lawyers, and maybe parents who would see to it that their daughter was released on bail during the first hearing. "Let's go."

She's got a one-way ticket to Cancun. Trust me, no judge would give that young woman bail. Her entire intent to commit the crime was predicated on escaping the country.

Leo and I remained by the cash register as everyone began to leave the shop. Liam escorted Bonnie across the street, while Cora had immediately taken a right on the sidewalk. No doubt she was calling her husband with the bad news. Or good news, depending on how one looked at the situation.

As for Bree, well…she was aiding her limping nephew in the opposite direction toward her car to take him into the city to have his ankle looked over. I'm sure we could expect a visit from her soon regarding the gourmet coffee inventory I was about to have on hand.

Ask for cash. By all that is Mother Nature, the woman certainly has a lot of it.

"We did good today, Leo," I murmured, a bit sad that my Valentine's Day plans had all but faded away. At least Paramour Bay was safe from a self-centered young woman who apparently never considered the consequences of her actions. "Looks like it's just you, me, and Ted tonight."

Ted had to cancel on me. Apparently, he's got dinner plans.

Liam and Bonnie had made it across the street. He opened the door to the station, and it wasn't long before both of them were out of sight.

"I wonder—"

Don't. It's better not to know.

Leo was right, but if Ted continued to have these mysterious dinner dates…let's just say Leo and I would have to do some investigating.

In the meantime, my phone was vibrating. It was probably Heidi asking which dress she should wear on her date with Jack tonight. I sighed in disappointment as I pulled my phone out of my skirt pocket. A shot of happiness streaked through me faster than the energy I had needed to pull for the spell.

A cantrip that I'd performed correctly, mind you.

You're actually celebrating the fact that you didn't have all of us boarding a plane to Lizard Island? Sweet angels of the supernatural, we have a lot of work ahead of us.

Ignore Leo. As you've read over the story, you can see for yourself that I'm getting better and better at all this magical stuff.

Anyway, I'm elated due to the fact that Liam texted me.

Guess what?

No.

"I wasn't talking to you," I grumbled, refusing to allow Leo's anticipated bad mood to ruin mine. "Liam just let me know that we're still on for tonight, but just not until after nine o'clock. Looks like we're heading home to prepare dinner and tidy up the house, Leo."

Oh, joy of joys. I feel a hairball coming on.

Shoot. Leo had just told me that his plans with Ted had fallen through, which meant he'd have to either spend the evening at home during my dinner with Liam or tag along with Ted. I guess Leo could have roamed around town for a bit or stayed at the tea shop, but I couldn't bring myself to suggest such a thing.

"Did I mention that I bought you a Valentine's Day present?"

Leo tilted his head to study my expression, but I was telling him the truth. It hadn't been easy keeping secrets from him, so I'd had to wait to look for his special gift during the times when he was asleep or taking a stroll around town.

Do I get a hint? I need to know if it's worth me staying at home to bear witness to a relationship that is doomed for failure.

I refused to believe that Liam and I would fail, especially given that things had been going good so far. The whole witch thing could remain under wraps given a reasonable amount of effort. Everyone had a small secret or two, right?

Small? We need to redefine your characterization of proportions.

"Leo, I promise that you're going to love your gift." I gave him a wink and went to collect my dress coat from the back. "Trust me."

Famous last words…

Chapter Twenty

THE DOORBELL RANG a little earlier than I'd expected, but I'd been able to get the house cleaned, store away all the magical components and ingredients I had on hand, and cook dinner to perfection. I had just finished tying a red scarf around my waist to give my black dress with the long bell sleeves an added bit of color and texture.

"Too bad Leo can't answer the door," I muttered to myself, coming down the spiral staircase that fed into the bedroom loft above the kitchen. Liam wasn't due for another twenty minutes, but he must have finished up earlier than expected. "Leo, how do I look?"

I'll let you know after you give me this gift you lured me with into staying for this fiasco.

"I'll get it in a second," I reassured him, not wanting to keep Liam waiting out in the cold on the front step. At least it was dark out so that stark branches of the vines growing out front weren't too visible. Come April, I'd have to enlist Ted to help me make the front of the yard presentable. "Coming!"

I hadn't wanted to go barefoot or wear my slippers for my date, so I'd put on a pair of ankle boots that had a higher heel than I was used to wearing. It probably wasn't the smartest thing to wear with my accident-prone tendencies.

If it stops you from opening that door…

Leo was busy cleaning himself in the middle of the window-sill, certainly giving Liam a show as he waited for me to open the door. Leo was trying to ignore that the next few hours would be spent entertaining Liam.

"Be nice," I warned, reaching out for the door handle with one last shooting glance at Leo. "I'm serious. Be on your best behavior."

I finally swung the door open with a bright smile on my face, completely taken aback by the man standing on my door step.

Wow. I didn't see that coming.

I had no doubt that if I'd glanced over at Leo that I would find his hind legs spread wide with his mouth hanging open in shock. I had to agree with him on the shock factor.

"Rye." Don't get me wrong. It had taken me at least five seconds to get my voice to work. "What are you doing here?"

I never thought I'd say this...but I'm glad the sheriff is about to pull up to the house. Now this is what I call a show.

"I heard about what happened with Bonnie, and I wanted to make sure you were okay." Rye had his hands in his coat pockets, but he'd used his elbow to indicate he'd been driving past. "I have to head into the city, and I saw your lights on. After you checking in on Gertie for me, I thought the least I could do was return the favor."

Please tell me that you're not buying this bullpucky.

I will admit that the palm of my hand sometimes tingled whenever Rye was around, but it was cool as a cucumber right now. I don't believe he posed a threat, and I wasn't the type of person to be mean for the sake of being mean.

Besides, Rye was giving me the most charming smile that made it hard to believe that he was being anything other than sincere.

He could be another Ted Bundy.

"I appreciate the gesture, Rye. I'm okay. Really," I reassured him with a smile of my own. It had been very sweet of him to go out of his way to make sure that I was okay, and in no way did Rye remind me of a serial killer. "The situation with Bonnie wasn't dangerous, but she is definitely in trouble for stealing money from the malt shop and setting all those fires around town."

It was quite awkward to stand in the middle of the doorway, allowing the cold air to enter the house. I'm sure Rye could see the candlelight dinner I'd set on the table, which made for an even more self-conscious moment. But he wasn't here in any other capacity than a friend, so inviting him in was the right thing to do.

Is it the right thing to do, Raven? Is it?

"I'm expecting Liam any moment, but would you like to come in?" I asked, ignoring the commentary from Leo. I was sure to get quite a bit of it tonight during dinner, but I was having a hard enough time dealing with this unexpected visit. In an odd way, I wasn't so sure how to act around Rye. "It's pretty cold out there tonight."

The man now has freezer burn after that letdown. Mentioning Liam was cold, Raven. I take back everything I said. Rye Dolgiram now looks like a lost puppy out in the rain. How could you be so mean?

"I appreciate the offer, but I was really just stopping by to make sure you were okay." Rye motioned once again to the main road. "I've got plans of my own in the city. Enjoy your evening, Raven."

Wait. Did he just ring the doorbell to snub you? I'm calling that a double gotcha.

I was left just inside the doorway to watch Rye walk back toward the gate, where his vehicle was waiting for him. I only just noticed the faint sound of the motor running, alerting me to the fact that he'd been telling the truth all along.

Rye had been here just to check on me, and I hadn't been the nicest of hosts. With that said, I found it odd that Rye would stop by the house when he'd never done so before, even with the excuse to make sure I was okay after today's confrontation with Bonnie.

Either that or he is *a serial killer who thought he could get away with dismembering your body without anyone the wiser. I just don't know which way to go!*

"He is not a serial killer," I grumbled underneath my breath, just in case Rye had good hearing. I kept a close eye on the man as he opened the gate, causing the hinges to do their thing and scream out in alarm that someone was touching it. "Uh-oh. He's looking back this way."

"Raven, I have some stuff in my truck that will take care of this for you," Rye called out, pointing to the hinges. "It won't take long, and then I'll be on my way."

I gradually closed the front door with a wave of thanks, not in any hurry to let him out of my sight. I mean, it wasn't an odd thing for a handyman to say, was it? He saw something wrong, and his immediate reaction was to fix it. Right?

That's a trick question, isn't it?

"I'm just finding it rather odd that Rye is being so nice after so many months of us keeping our distance from each other."

Did it ever occur to you that my theory about a serial killer is spot on, and that he's oiling up those hinges so that the next time he comes...you won't hear a thing?

"One, you and I both know that my right palm warns me at

any hint of danger," I reminded him, wishing I could look out the window without being caught. "Two, I've personally tried WD40 on those hinges, and nothing makes them shut up. The only one who can open the gate without a sound is Ted, which I have yet to figure out the reason why. I think Nan put a ward on it to give an alert of anyone approaching. Ted doesn't trigger the alert because he isn't human."

I ran my hands up and down my arms to gain a bit of warmth now that the cold was finally dissipating. Maybe I should add a log to the fire. Liam would be here any second, and I wanted everything to be perfect. It didn't take me long to feed the flames and have the additional heat radiating from the fire at the perfect temperature.

"Leo, are you sure you wouldn't rather spend the evening at—"

I would have finished my question had I not caught sight of Leo looking like he'd seen a ghost. Trust me, we'd encountered one before. I remember the exact moment Leo's gaze had landed on the spry Mazie Rose Young in her otherworldly form—which had included a delicate teacup and a pink floppy hat. No one could say that she hadn't gone out in style.

"Leo, what's wrong?" I began to make my way over to him when the doorbell rang. Was he pulling some type of prank where I flung open the door and expected Rye, but in reality, it was Liam? Or had Rye returned? "I'm not falling for it. Rye should have left by now, and Liam is due any second."

Do you think that catnip can cause hallucinations?

"No. Well, maybe. Dr. Jameson didn't say anything about the catnip other than you couldn't overdose on the stuff."

I wrapped my hand around the door handle once more.

Then we have a problem.

I'd even turned the handle, letting whoever was on the other side know that I was at the door. But how did Leo expect me to conduct myself with composure when there was obviously a problem somewhere?

"Leo, you better tell me now." I wanted everything out in the open so that I wasn't preoccupied during dinner. "Spill it!"

I think Rye Dolgiram might be a… No. No, forget I said anything.

I wonder if there was a way to travel back in time to find out what Leo had seen through the window. Could there be a spell somewhere in the grimoire?

"Don't answer that," I warned, swinging the door open before I could change my mind. There was nothing I could do about this tidbit of information now, and nothing—I repeat, nothing—was going to ruin this Valentine's Day dinner. "Liam! Oh, my goodness! They are absolutely beautiful."

The dozen red roses that Liam was carrying in a beautiful red vase was beyond stunning in their arrangement. There were even those baby breaths sprinkled throughout the blooms, giving an appearance that was simply breathtaking.

No pun intended, right? Hey, listen. Maybe I did hallucinate Rye…well, do what he did. I mean, what are the odds that he's some type of… Never mind. Seriously, let's just forget I ever said anything, okay?

I was beginning to think that Leo had learned to protest a bit too much, similar to what he'd accused me of earlier in the story.

There is only so much drama I can take, and I've reached my quota today. Hey, can I get my gift now? I'm beginning to think you made that up so I wouldn't be mad that I was stuck here with the two of you.

"Raven, it is you who looks absolutely beautiful," Liam

claimed, taking in my outfit that I'd so painstakingly changed my mind about every ten seconds until I'd found the red scarf. His dark eyes practically caressed me, and I realized that this was how Valentine's Day should be spent—with someone who appreciated me as much as I appreciated them. "Happy Valentine's Day."

Liam had yet to let go of the vase that I had wrapped my hand around, but instead used it to draw me closer. I accepted his kiss, causing a warmth inside of me that the hearth could never generate.

It's going to be a long night, isn't it?

"Thank you for changing the time on our dinner plans." Liam finally stepped over the threshold and closed the door behind him. Honestly, I hadn't even noticed the cold. "The booking process and paperwork didn't take long, especially once Bonnie's lawyer was called. She now resides in a holding cell in a proper city jail. The county sheriff was kind enough to transfer her for me."

I had taken the vase when Liam had closed the door. As much as the roses would make the perfect centerpiece on the dining room table, I wanted to be able to see Liam while we ate. The coffee table would have to do, and I gave Leo a warning glance that he should leave them alone. He had a propensity to knock things over when he didn't feel he was getting enough attention.

Lies. All lies. The masses are nothing if not jealous.

"I still can't believe that Bonnie was the one who started those fires all to hide the fact that she was stealing from the malt shop." I stepped back around the couch, but Liam had already taken off his suede jacket and hung it up on the antique coat rack. I'd swear his black sweater was cashmere, but I didn't want to make a fool of myself by running my fingers down the fabric. "I've already opened a bottle of wine, if that's okay."

I'll just sit here and debate if I'm losing my mind. It's okay. Just ignore me. I'll play the "she got me a gift, she didn't get me a gift" game with my...hey, didn't I have seventeen claws at the beginning of this story?

"I think we both deserve a drink after a day like today," Liam agreed, following me across the hardwood floor. He took a seat at the counter, leaning back on the stool and watching me as I began to pour the open bottle of red wine. I was quite proud of myself that I didn't spill any, especially with my accident-prone tendencies. "We made quite a team. You kept everyone calm, which was quite a feat considering Cora has a tendency to dramatize any situation."

"I think she was too stunned by what was taking place to make it all about her." Today had gone smoothly, and this was the perfect way to end a very chaotic week. I slid Liam's wineglass closer to him while lifting my own. "Here's to solving another mystery."

What am I? Chopped liver?

Liam showed me that sexy grin of his, only lifting one corner to say he found my toast amusing.

"I think you're the mystery that needs solving, Raven Lattice Marigold."

I wiggled my eyebrows as I took a delicious sip of the red wine, telling myself it was okay to keep Liam guessing. That sort of thing made for an exciting relationship, right?

"Oh!" I exclaimed, having almost forgotten my promise to Leo. "I'm sorry. I almost forgot to give a small Valentine's Day present to Leo."

I knew you forgot.

I turned on my black heels and opened up the cupboard where I'd stored Leo's gift. I'd had to seal the area with a spell to make sure Leo hadn't caught a whiff of the all-natural Black Forest grown catnip I'd ordered.

I leaned in close to Liam as I walked past, having him play along. He was a good sport about Leo and my eccentricities.

"Trust me, it will keep him busy while we enjoy our evening together."

I heard that.

I continued to smile as I walked up to Leo, who had thankfully closed his hind legs after finishing his bath. At least he was showing some measure of decorum this evening.

"Here you go," I whispered, setting down the fresh grown plant that was in a heart-shaped white planter. The green blades were healthy and sticking straight up one by one. "This is an all-natural catnip grown in the deepest, darkest glades of the German Black Forest. It is as exclusive as you're going to get, my friend."

You...you bought me a real live imported catnip plant. Look at it. It's...beautiful.

Leo had used his two front legs to push himself back on his haunches, his larger left eye staring at the gift as if he'd never seen anything so delicious. It warmed my heart to be able to give him something back.

And for once, it seemed as if I'd made Leo somewhat speechless. Trust me, that was a feat unto itself. As a matter of fact, I was quite proud of myself.

"You're my partner in crime. No matter who may come or go in my life, you're my constant." I planted a gentle kiss on his forehead. "Happy Valentine's Day, Leo."

That literally should have been the last line at the end of this book. My quiet evening with Liam should have commenced without another hiccup, and I would have had wonderful memories to share with you in our next story.

Unfortunately, I was going to have to work a little bit harder on my goal of making Leo speechless. Honestly, I was lucky I didn't trip in these high heels at the shocking revelation he just couldn't keep to himself for only a few more hours. I mean, that hadn't been asking for much, right?

Is now a good time to tell you that I think Rye Dolgiram is a warlock?

~ THE END ~

Thank you so much for reading Charming Blend! And don't worry, there are more shenanigans ahead for Raven and Leo. Spellbinding Blend is the next cozy mystery this comical duo must solve, and you can read all about it below!

kennedylayne.com/spellbinding-blend.html

This is one spellbinding tale of magical chaos you won't want to miss in the continuation of USA Today Bestselling Author Kennedy Layne's cozy paranormal mystery series...

The flowers are in bloom, the songbirds are singing, and the tourists have begun to flock to the small coastal town of Paramour Bay for the Spring Festival. All is going according to plan, but Raven Marigold has one itsy-bitsy loose end to tie up regarding a possible warlock posing as one of the townsfolk. There has to be a simple solution, right?

Well, one itsy-bitsy loose end turns into two...maybe three...when a body is found behind the kissing booth at the traveling carnival on the edge of town. When Raven discovers a connection between the victim and the warlock she's been keeping a close eye on, she and her trusty familiar will have no choice but to take the case. After all, it wouldn't do to have the residents know that magic exists!

Grab a ticket and take a ride on this swirling mystery that will leave you dizzy with misleading clues, magical chaos, and a spellbinding blend that doesn't quite go according to plan!

Books by Kennedy Layne

Paramour Bay Mysteries

Magical Blend

Bewitching Blend

Enchanting Blend

Haunting Blend

Charming Blend

Spellbinding Blend

Office Roulette Series

Means (Office Roulette, Book One)

Motive (Office Roulette, Book Two)

Opportunity (Office Roulette, Book Three)

Keys to Love Series

Unlocking Fear (Keys to Love, Book One)

Unlocking Secrets (Keys to Love, Book Two)

Unlocking Lies (Keys to Love, Book Three)

Unlocking Shadows (Keys to Love, Book Four)

Unlocking Darkness (Keys to Love, Book Five)

Surviving Ashes Series

Essential Beginnings (Surviving Ashes, Book One)

Hidden Ashes (Surviving Ashes, Book Two)

Buried Flames (Surviving Ashes, Book Three)

Endless Flames (Surviving Ashes, Book Four)

Rising Flames (Surviving Ashes, Book Five)

CSA Case Files Series

Captured Innocence (CSA Case Files 1)

Sinful Resurrection (CSA Case Files 2)

Renewed Faith (CSA Case Files 3)

Campaign of Desire (CSA Case Files 4)

Internal Temptation (CSA Case Files 5)

Radiant Surrender (CSA Case Files 6)

Redeem My Heart (CSA Case Files 7)

A Mission of Love (CSA Case Files 8)

Red Starr Series

Starr's Awakening(Red Starr, Book One)

Hearths of Fire (Red Starr, Book Two)

Targets Entangled (Red Starr, Book Three)

Igniting Passion (Red Starr, Book Four)

Untold Devotion (Red Starr, Book Five)

Fulfilling Promises (Red Starr, Book Six)

Fated Identity (Red Starr, Book Seven)

Red's Salvation (Red Starr, Book Eight)

The Safeguard Series

Brutal Obsession (The Safeguard Series, Book One)

Faithful Addiction (The Safeguard Series, Book Two)

Distant Illusions (The Safeguard Series, Book Three)

Casual Impressions (The Safeguard Series, Book Four)

Honest Intentions (The Safeguard Series, Book Five)

Deadly Premonitions (The Safeguard Series, Book Six)

ABOUT THE AUTHOR

First and foremost, I love life. I love that I'm a wife, mother, daughter, sister… and a writer.

I am one of the lucky women in this world who gets to do what makes them happy. As long as I have a cup of coffee (maybe two or three) and my laptop, the stories evolve themselves and I try to do them justice. I draw my inspiration from a retired Marine Master Sergeant that swept me off of my feet and has drawn me into a world that fulfills all of my deepest and darkest desires. Erotic romance, military men, intrigue, with a little bit of kinky chili pepper (his recipe), fill my head and there is nothing more satisfying than making the hero and heroine fulfill their destinies.

Thank you for having joined me on their journeys…

Email: kennedylayneauthor@gmail.com

Facebook: facebook.com/kennedy.layne.94

Twitter: twitter.com/KennedyL_Author

Website: www.kennedylayne.com

Newsletter:

www.kennedylayne.com/aboutnewsletter.html

Made in the USA
Coppell, TX
27 May 2020

26334713R00105